"I wanted to go to you that night at the opera, to kiss you right there, to touch your emerald earrings, which were as close to you as I wanted to be. Do you ever want me half as much, Micah?" Chance demanded.

She felt herself yielding to him.

"Do you remember our kisses, our lovemaking, and relive it all over again? he asked. "I do. I've replayed them in my mind until they're as much a part of me as breathing. I only wish I knew you felt the same way. That's all I ask for now, nothing more. Tell me if you still want me, and I promise to leave it at that."

His hand caressed her cheek as he spoke, and when he finished, she turned her face until her lips were nestled in his palm. She kissed his hand gently. "I want you, Chance. I've never really wanted anyone but you. I've cried at night from wanting you so much."

He took the gamble. "Then want me more. If I so much as kiss you again, it'll be only because you ask for it. Not before. You wanted space, and so help me, I'm going to give it to you. When you're ready, I'll be waiting." He drew her into his embrace, and for a few moments he trusted himself to hold her. "Goodnight, Micah," he murmured, then turned away and took two steps.

"Chance," she whispered. "Kiss me."

WHAT ARE *LOVESWEPT* ROMANCES?

They are stories of true romance and touching emotion. We believe those two very important ingredients are constants in our highly sensual and very believable stories in the *LOVESWEPT* line. Our goal is to give you, the reader, stories of consistently high quality that may sometimes make you laugh, sometimes make you cry, but are always fresh and creative and contain many delightful surprises within their pages.

Most romance fans read an enormous number of books. Those they truly love, they keep. Others may be traded with friends and soon forgotten. We hope that each *LOVESWEPT* romance will be a treasure—a "keeper." We will always try to publish

LOVE STORIES YOU'LL NEVER FORGET
BY AUTHORS YOU'LL ALWAYS REMEMBER

The Editors

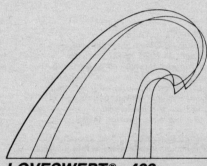

LOVESWEPT® • 428

Olivia M. Rupprecht
Bad Boy of New Orleans

 BANTAM BOOKS
NEW YORK • TORONTO • LONDON • SYDNEY • AUCKLAND

BAD BOY OF NEW ORLEANS

A Bantam Book / October 1990

LOVESWEPT® and the wave device are registered
trademarks of Bantam Books, a division of
Bantam Doubleday Dell Publishing Group, Inc.
Registered in U.S. Patent
and Trademark Office and elsewhere.

If you would be interested in receiving protective vinyl cov-
ers for your Loveswept books, please write to this address
for information:

> Loveswept
> Bantam Books
> P. O. Box 985
> Hicksville, NY 11802

ISBN 0-553-44059-4

Published simultaneously in the United States and Canada

Bantam Books are published by Bantam Books, a division
of Bantam Doubleday Dell Publishing Group, Inc. Its trade-
mark, consisting of the words "Bantam Books" and the
portrayal of a rooster, is Registered in U.S. Patent and
Trademark Office and in other countries. Marca Regis-
trada. Bantam Books, 666 Fifth Avenue, New York, New
York 10103.

PRINTED IN THE UNITED STATES OF AMERICA

OPM   0 9 8 7 6 5 4 3 2 1

For Scott,
A hero, if ever there was.

One

The flowers hadn't arrived yet. Micah checked the clock again—9:00 A.M.—where *were* they? Maybe she should call the florist to make sure they hadn't forgotten . . .

Don't be ridiculous, she chided herself. After all, she didn't even *order* the flowers, they just came, like clockwork every day for the past month.

Micah plucked at the white blouse that clung with humid tenacity to her skin and stole another glance out the leaded glass window. Still no flowers—except for the azalea bushes and magnolia trees, and they didn't count. Everyone in New Orleans owned some of those. Early May transformed even the plainest homes into perfume paradises of fuschia and white blooms.

She sighed and forced herself away from the window and back to the dog-eared section of the want ads.

Today was grimmer than usual.

She scratched out a receptionist position she'd

circled earlier. Typing was required. She was pretty sure twenty words per minute probably wouldn't cut it. She continued down the column until she reached the *W's*.

"Waitress," she muttered. She poised the pen, then read on: "Must have background in serving etiquette for prestigious establishment."

She had etiquette, but not *serving* etiquette. She sighed and pitched the paper into the ornate fireplace. Nothing today. Again.

From outside she heard the sound of an engine's sustained rumble. Micah jumped off the worn Victorian sofa and dashed to the window.

The flowers! They were here! She hadn't realized how much she looked forward to them until she thought the mysterious sender had forgotten her.

Long ingrained rules dictated she wait patiently until the delivery man knocked on the door.

"Hi, Theo!" she called from the veranda as the teenager alighted from the driver's seat. "I was almost getting worried that you weren't coming today. Need some help getting that out?"

" 'Afternoon, Ms. Sinclair. Thanks for the offer, but I can handle it. Got you a big one today. 'Fraid that's why I was running so late. Those little posies were one thing, but *this*. Why, you're not gonna believe it." He opened the side door and leaned in. "Someone must really think a lot of you. Why, they even sent this fancy crystal container over to put them in. Good thing. We didn't have anything big enough to hold it all."

He turned around and Micah gasped. She was

at the gate, and held onto the black iron grille work to support herself.

"Oh, my word," she breathed. "Who in the world—"

"Reckon you might be about to find out. This one has a card attached."

"A card? You mean I finally get a card?" Micah fought the urge to scramble through the arrangement to snatch it.

"The messenger who brought the big vase said to be sure to enclose the note. It was sealed nice and tight."

She led him into the house and over to the entry table before quickly gathering up the plumed quill and guest book to make space. Theo carefully set down his burden, gave a once-over to the surroundings, and sniffed.

"Not that we mind the business, Ms. Sinclair, but this place is starting to look more like a wedding hall or a funeral parlor—" His face turned beet-red before he rushed on, "I'm sorry . . . I didn't mean to—"

"Don't feel bad, Theo. You didn't upset me."

"Well . . . it's only been a month. I know you're still mourning . . . and . . ." He ducked his head. "Well, you know what I mean."

She felt like a fraud. Keeping up the pretense of mourning was tough, and poor Theo had been her daily dupe. Ever since he'd delivered several of the funeral sprays then followed those up the next day with a single red rose minus a card. She remembered how he'd mumbled his personal condolences even though they were strangers. The memory made her feel doubly guilty now.

"Of course I know what you mean. Now take this for my thanks and go see a movie with your girl." She took out a ten hidden in the back of the guest book and pressed it into his hand. Micah tried not to think about how low her gas tank was. "After all, you deserve it for hauling that botanical garden over here."

When he tried to refuse, she shooed him out the door.

At last! She turned her attention to the fragrance tantalizing her nostrils. It was the scent of curiosity more than the exotic bouquet drawing her near.

Micah stretched her anticipation to the limit. So little to look forward to these days, she relished the small intrigue. As she touched gardenias, bird of paradise, and several varieties of orchids, she eyed the tempting envelope beneath the petal of an orange tiger lily.

Once opened, she had to go back to the dismal prospects awaiting her attention in the fireplace.

All the better to make this last; play a game with no rules beyond her imagination. A game she'd been playing from the single red rose to the potted philodendron to the daisies and baby's breath to . . . *this*. A celebration bouquet.

Now . . . who could it be? They had to come from the same person. After all, how many people would send thirty arrangements without so much as a note? It had to be someone who realized she loved flowers more than chocolate. Someone who knew her well enough not to send a note since she would have called with her thanks but refused such extravagance after a few bouquets. A person who might know she was going crazy by mid-morning without even the comfort of work to lose herself in, and who made sure they came before noon each day.

Micah glided a fingertip over the envelope, then plucked it from the mauve satin bow. Could it be an aunt or cousin, some other relation? Not likely. She was almost shunned as a black sheep after losing most of her inheritance.

Perhaps a business associate? She owed most of them money.

Maybe one of the charities to which she belonged? They were usually after her for more donations, and lately she hadn't had any to contribute.

Then, it had to be one of the good-hearted matrons whom she'd known all her life in the social arena. Only they had stopped calling and bringing covered dishes over two weeks ago.

A last possibility emerged. One she tried to shut out each time she played this little game. She usually managed to ignore the way he constantly hovered on the fringes of her every waking moment. But as always he didn't fight fair. He came to her at night, penetrating her dreams.

Suddenly the game was no longer fun. Her hands felt damper than the shirt clinging to her skin, and she fumbled awkwardly getting the message out.

Her mouth went dry. Her unsteady hand lost its grip of the card, and she watched in paralytic fascination as the familiar handwriting sailed awkwardly to the polished oak floor. Micah hesitated, wondering if she was wise to even touch the note again.

She couldn't just leave it there. "Pick it up," she ordered herself. "Pick it up. Throw it away. Along with the flowers."

She bent down, her movements jerky as a marionette on a string. When her fingers brushed over the paper, a rush of forbidden excitement swept through to heat each cell of her body. Her eyes were drawn uncontrollably to the words she'd memorized at first glance:

Flowers are for the living, not the dead.
You know where to find me.

                              Chance

She began to rip the card in half, as though she could banish the man as easily. The paper sighed as she tore at it, but before it was half-done, she stopped.

She touched the flare of his signature. She pressed her lips against the boldness of his message.

Chance Renault. Some people said he'd traded his soul for his fortune, and knowing Chance, she wouldn't be surprised. Chance was too ambitious, too single-minded. Word was, he didn't possess a single scruple.

She could almost believe it of him. Once, he'd made her almost believe it of herself. For her, Chance was as addictive as an illegal drug—dangerous, forbidden, a poison her system craved.

She knew she wouldn't throw the card away.

She would take it and hide it in her drawer where she couldn't see the temptation it represented.

She turned toward the stairs leading to the bedroom, but caught sight of herself in the entry mirror. Her cheeks were flushed with color, and there was a glow that was almost radiance in her face. Disgusted with herself, she turned abruptly away, determined not to smell the flowers again. She proved her strength by not even looking at them.

Halfway up the landing, Micah stopped. She tried, she really did. But as though her body had a will all its own, she did a quarter turn.

Just far enough to thrill once more to the ominous beauty of the celebration bouquet.

Chance sat in the driver's seat of his sleek black Lamborghini. The engine idled in a companionable silence while he stared out the darkly tinted window toward the front veranda of Micah's century-old house. He noticed it needed some fresh paint.

"The grieving widow," Chance muttered to himself.

The door opened and Micah stood there, poised for a moment, as though she sensed his presence. Chance knew he should leave before she spotted him, especially since he'd sworn to wait her out. Except he'd been waiting over a month, and the daily flowers didn't seem to be luring her closer, the way they were meant to. Besides, she looked too good in the gauzy tropical sundress to tear his eyes away from the creamy skin which, even from a distance, made his fingers itch to touch.

He turned off the ignition, and let the car go dead. Leaving would be smart. But when he thought of Micah, his smarts—street and otherwise—didn't seem to exist.

She'd been doing that to him for a very long time. Long before she'd hooked up with Jonathon, that gutless wonder of a husband who had finally had the decency to kick off and save Micah the pain of a nasty divorce. Unfortunately he'd left a mess behind for her to clean up anyway.

Micah was rummaging in her purse now, probably looking for her car keys, Chance guessed. Her silky black hair was coming loose from the clasp he knew she usually wore. He wished she would just let it fall loose—over her shoulders, around her sweet, open face. The one that now seemed so strained, so anxious. Even from a distance he could see a pinched look around her eyes. Usually a sparkling jade, they seemed tired, not hers at all.

Chance's fingers tightened around the steering wheel, and his jaw clenched with anger. The bastard. How he hated that man. Not only for taking what should have been his, but for not having had the decency to at least take care of her once he did have her; for gambling her security away.

Chance knew he was no angel himself; he had his own share of favorite vices. With money to burn, he had discovered poker was a pleasant enough way to play with it. Carefully, of course—he'd done without too long to risk losing much. But he was good, and certainly didn't mind lightening someone else's pockets.

Anyone's, really. Except for Jonathon's. Because

Jonathon had oozed and lost the last of both his and Micah's inherited money, Chance had always felt distaste when he took Jonathon on in a card game. He wouldn't have stooped to playing with him, except the only way to pick up bits and pieces of information on Micah was when Jonathon's tongue loosened from too much booze.

More than once he'd used every shred of willpower he possessed not to jump across the table to get at the drunken slob for making some off-handed comment about her. Only one thing was worse. The sick feeling he got every time Jonathon left for the night. Home to Micah. Home, where he had the legal right to touch her and make love to her, to be all the things that Chance longed to be.

Now he was dead. Chance grinned mirthlessly as he mused that by plunging off a narrow bridge and drowning in the car, Jonathon had died with more style than he'd lived. That should mean Micah had double indemnity coming her way with the insurance, and Lord knew she probably deserved—and needed—every penny.

She was halfway to the carriage house where she kept her car, bypassing the fuchsia blooms of azalea bushes without bending to smell them as she usually did when he was watching. He studied her as she walked, the hurried way she passed through the black grille work of the iron gate surrounding the house. As Micah got into her car, an older model BMW, Chance idly wondered how many more miles she had left in the thing.

Before he gave himself time to think about it,

he turned on the ignition. With perfect timing he backed up until he blocked the driveway just as she pulled out of the carriage house to navigate her way down the narrow strip of asphalt.

Chance climbed out of his car, knowing she'd seen him. He saw her hesitate and wondered if she would simply head back to the carriage house. He felt sure Micah was a little afraid of being alone with him. *Smart lady,* he thought.

He leaned back against the car, casually crossing his arms. He fixed her with a steady, mocking stare and waited to see if she would rise to the silent challenge.

Micah held her breath until her lungs felt as if they might burst from the pressure. Her skin prickled as Chance continued to watch her with a cool, predatory stance that belonged solely to him. Even in his tailored suit he looked like a man who would be more at home in a leather jacket. A black one—to match his dark, brooding features, his cutting edge presence.

She felt a sudden impulse to gun the car forward, fast enough to burn rubber. Instead, she reached for the handle to let herself out, hating the way her hands were suddenly damp, the way they trembled. Her legs weren't doing much better as she approached him. She held her back erect though, and fixed what she hoped was a stern expression on her face.

"Chance." She greeted him warily.

"Glad you decided to stay, Micah."

Damn him anyway, she felt like screaming.

Couldn't he have the decency to stay away from new widows? And couldn't he look just a little less cocky, a little less blatantly sure of his masculine prowess?

"It is my driveway, Chance." She managed to sound in control, and was proud of herself for that. "Were you ready to leave?"

Chance didn't flinch or raise an eyebrow. "Nice try, Micah. But I don't buy it. Why don't we get the preliminaries over with? Say you'll see me Saturday night, then we can talk."

"You seem to forget that I'm in mourning. Jonathon's only been gone six weeks, Chance. Can't you show a little respect?"

Chance pushed away from his car and came closer. Micah could feel her heart begin to race even faster, and for a horrifying moment she thought she was going to hyperventilate in front of him. Micah took a self-protective step back, and then another, and another until she backed herself against the BMW. She reached for the handle behind her, not quite sure what she meant to do.

He quickly closed the small distance and propped his arm beside her on the roof of the car. "Respect?" Chance's voice was smooth. "You know I respect you."

"That's not what I meant and you know it," she retorted, flustered now.

"Come on, Micah," Chance said, his voice holding a trace of bitterness. "He was a sorry excuse for a man and you know it." He cocked his head as though expecting a reaction, but when she looked away, he went on relentlessly.

"In fact, I'm curious. Tell me what kind of legacy he left you now that his gambling buddies have had a chance to come collect their debts."

Micah drew her breath in sharply. "That's none of your business," she snapped. "And *I* am none of your business. Leave me alone, Chance. Go toy with someone who wants to play your games."

Micah tried to fling the car door open, to make him step away. Chance caught the door and slammed it shut. His hand was braced against it, and Micah couldn't seem to tear her gaze away from the leashed strength of his arm, the near mahogany color of his sun-glazed skin, the rough, dark hair covering his wrist. Chance caught her chin with his free hand and made her look at him. She tried to flinch away from his touch. A touch she couldn't wipe out, no matter how hard she tried to forget she had succumbed to it years ago. She thrilled to it even now.

"Toy? Games?" he repeated in a low voice. "I'm disappointed in you, Micah. Because if one of us is guilty of playing games, it's you. Now face the truth and admit it. You want to see me, you *need* to see me, as much as I—" He stopped suddenly, his fist striking a soft blow against the top of her car. "*Damn.* If you'd only waited when I asked, we would have happened a long time ago. We've lost too many years already. I'm not willing to lose any more."

He wasn't hurting her, but the subdued force of his hand was intimidating, and strangely exciting. So were his words. She didn't hear the accusation in them she'd expected, but the underlying command was just short of domination. The force of his touch, his nearness, his penetrating gaze boring into hers suddenly threatened to swallow her whole.

In a surge of self-protection Micah jerked her chin away, refusing to meet his eyes a moment longer.

"Please leave."

"Look at me and say that, then maybe I'll believe you."

Micah forced her eyes to meet his once more for a brief, agonizing moment. "The answer is *no*," she said, her voice sounding like a plea in her own ears.

"You *say* no. Why do I get the feeling you're lying to me? To yourself? Don't ever try to take deception up for a living, Micah. You're lousy at it."

"Too bad you're not."

Micah regretted the words as soon as they were out. For so brief an instant she wondered if she had imagined it, she could have sworn she saw him grimace.

"He really did a number on you, didn't he?" Chance laughed then, a little unpleasantly, and she decided the moment of vulnerability had been in her imagination after all.

Before she could reply, Chance reached down and opened the door, stepping back to swing it out. She got in quickly, needing to get away as fast as she could before doing something totally insane—like giving into the urgent voice, the one without reason, that cried out for her to take the risk.

Chance bent down so his head was level with

hers. "A little more time, Micah? I've waited years, what's a few more weeks?"

He studied her face then, and Micah did her best to shut him out, not to acknowledge the exhilaration that came with his nearness, or the acute, unwanted things he was doing to her inside and out. She felt confined by her own emotions, and the tension between them was stretched so taut, she expected to hear something snap.

Then for a frozen, heart-stopping moment he bent close as though he meant to kiss her.

Micah heard her own breath hiss through her teeth as Chance fastened her seat belt.

"You can run, Micah," he whispered, his face scant inches from hers. "You can run as fast and as hard as those sweet, long legs can take you, but in the end you'll still run to me. Because I'll be there every which way you turn. And Micah," he touched her cheek with the tips of his fingers, and she felt the jolt of that touch down to the pit of her stomach. "Remember. When you've got no one else to go to, you know where to find me."

Micah couldn't bear to look into his searching gaze a moment longer. She shut her eyes against him and turned the key hard in the ignition, revving the engine.

She heard the heavy thud of his own door over the throbbing pulse pounding against her temples. His engine purred, and she opened her eyes against her will, stealing a last, furtive glance in the rearview mirror. His darkened window slid down in a smooth, gliding motion. Too quick for her to look away, he tilted his head and raised a brow. Then with a casual wave he took off in his sleek black car.

A Lamborghini, she reflected wryly. It suited the man—fast and used to owning the road, nudging out anything that got in its way.

Like Chance.

He had been known to be cruel, ruthless. A man, Micah thought, who some believed had no capacity for tenderness, for love. She could almost believe that, although she knew otherwise. She *needed* to believe that, and she could. As long as she didn't remember . . .

Two

Ian Fields peered at her over the rim of his bifocals, his pot belly hidden behind the mammoth banker's desk. Micah sat in silence while his voice droned on from what seemed a very great distance. She was relieved that his shocking news had at least stunned the tears right out of her.

"I'm sorry, Ian. Did you ask me something?"

"I asked if you had a job yet?"

She shook her head and laughed with a cynicism that wasn't in her nature. "I've been looking. There seems to be a shortage of jobs for sociology majors without any experience. Or 'purveyors of fine antiques' whose century-old family business went belly up five years after she inherited it. Other than that, social position and volunteer work don't seem to count for much in the employment line."

Ian wrinkled his forehead in concentration. "Do you type? Take dictation? Any secretarial experience?"

She blew the air between her lips in a sound of disgust. "If I could have a dollar for every time I've been asked that question in the last month, I wouldn't be asking you for a loan. And I wouldn't be trying to start my own business."

"Collateral?"

"Just what's on the loan application—my car. I didn't want to list the house." Micah almost wished he'd ordered her out the door several minutes ago. At least then she wouldn't have to endure this conversation.

"That's good. After all, it did belong to your grandparents, and the bank could take it away if you didn't make your payments."

"Which apparently makes no difference either way. You won't lend me the money."

Slowly, firmly, Ian shook his head. "As hard as it is for me to be telling you this, it's just the facts. A bank is a business, not a charity."

Micah cleared her throat, the word trying to crawl its way back up. *Charity. She,* who hadn't dreamed of asking for anything once in her whole life, who had been raised to wear her pride like a mantle of honor—*she* did *not* take charity.

Abruptly she stood up, grabbing her purse off the floor. Very stiffly, Micah offered her hand. Ian rose to his feet and accepted the brief handshake, visibly relieved she was leaving.

"Thank you, Mr. Fields. I believe you've made your position quite clear, so I won't take up any more of your time. Good day."

She swung around, her back as rigid as a military cadet's, and started for the door.

"Micah, wait! Don't leave like this." Ian came

around the desk as quickly as his girth allowed. He caught up with her and placed a restraining hand over her arm. "Maybe we could work something out. A personal loan . . . some kind of understanding between us."

She *must* have misunderstood him, misinterpreted the inflection in his voice that sent instinctive chills of revulsion up her spine. Then she looked down at his pudgy hand stroking her arm and removed it from his touch with a feeling of utter disgust. She risked a glance into his face, hoping to see the jovial, benign old man she had known for so long, wanting to find that she had imagined the whole episode.

Something glittered behind the glasses he wore. It was a look that even in her limited experience Micah recognized.

"Keep the loan," she said coldly, though she couldn't keep her voice from shaking. "I don't take charity. And I'm not collateral."

Quickly then, Micah strode out the door and closed it firmly behind her.

"I can handle this," she said aloud to herself. What had just happened, didn't happen. It couldn't have.

Although she knew it had.

She hurried on, wanting to get away as quickly as possible.

Several people greeted her, but the best she could do was nod her head while she kept walking fast, then faster, trying not to think any further than reaching her car.

"Micah."

Chance.

She quickened her pace, unable to look at him, much less return his greeting.

He grabbed her arm and brought her up short.

"Let go, Chance." The anger, the anguish was too close to the surface, and right now she didn't even care if he heard it.

"Did you hear me?" she said through clenched teeth. "I said, 'Let . . . Go.' "

An immediate, uncanny understanding registered in his eyes. "What happened?" he demanded gruffly.

"What happened? Oh, nothing. Just that I found out Jonathon withdrew the last of my inheritance the week before he died. Just that he had credit and I didn't because I was too naive, too *damned* ignorant to realize I had to sign some stupid papers to—"

"Micah, don't." His voice was firm but quiet, a commanding contrast to her rising rage.

"Don't what?" she flung out, managing to keep her voice lowered in spite of the urge to yell. "Don't get upset because it makes no difference I've had an account here for years, or that my parents, even my grandparents, did business with these . . . these *jerks* before I was even born? Oh, and let's not forget that above all, this *is* a *business. Not* a *charity.*"

Chance at least had the decency to appear stunned. And then she noticed he hadn't let go yet. In fact, he was tightening his hold and starting to escort her out of the bank as he spoke with a concern that even in her agitated state was unmistakable.

"For the love of . . . Micah, what in the world

happened in there? I've never seen you so upset. So help me, if anyone's been mistreating you, I'll—"

"You'll what? Punch their lights out? Withdraw your money and give up your seat on the board of directors? Save yourself the trouble, Chance. It won't make a damned bit of difference. The only thing that's going to change is *me*."

They were outside and she whirled around, palm flush against her chest. Her eyes snapped emerald fire, and without the restraint of an audience, she gave in to the impulse to raise her voice.

"Look at me, Chance. Twenty-eight years old, and with nothing to show for it. I've got less now than I had ten years ago. Well, I'm tired of going through life like a helpless, simpering fool without the ability to stand on my own two feet— needing my family, or a man to keep me financially secure. And obviously there's plenty out there happy to do just that as long as I'm willing to pay with interest. Not money, of course. Just sexual favors."

Chance's features changed before her eyes. Something very hard and mean and dark was carved into his face, as though he was suddenly cast in granite.

"Has some man tried to come on to you like that?" he demanded harshly.

"I—" Her voice dropped to a whisper.

Caution sounded in her head. Chance was ready to make an ugly situation into a field of carnage. He wouldn't just tell Ian to back off, he'd draw blood then drown him in it. As much as she'd like to see Ian brought to task, she would not be responsible for his ruin.

"Answer me, Micah." Chance caught her arms in a steely grip and brought his face close to hers. His brows were drawn together and his teeth were clenched.

"No," she said. "No one. I was just upset, that's all."

"I don't believe you. If someone's been hitting on you, you'd better tell me. *Now*."

"I don't have to tell you anything, Chance Renault. Now take your hands off me, because if anyone's been hitting on me, it's you."

This time he flinched, Micah was sure of it. She had wronged him, and she knew it. She felt herself cringe inside for hurting this man she had loved above all others. This man she must now avoid above all others.

"I'll see you to your car," he said in a tight voice. "Where are you parked?"

Micah looked away, unable to meet his gaze a moment longer. She saw her BMW a few cars down, and Chance followed her train of vision.

He loosened his hold and led her over to her car in silence.

Micah let herself in, still not risking another glance at Chance.

"When you're through being mad at the world in general," he said, leaning down, "and me in particular, call me. Or come see me. Morning, evening, middle of the night. I don't care when, because I'll be waiting. For you, Micah. It's always been you, and no matter how many times you turn me away, I'll never forget the way your mouth tastes, or how it felt when you took me inside and wrapped your legs around me and told me you loved me."

She gasped, suddenly speechless.

"I thought that would get your attention." She looked away quickly, and his face hardened with resolution.

"Oh, you can try to forget it, Micah. You can pretend it never happened. But it did. It was the best thing that had ever happened to me then, and nothing's come close since. Only don't take too much longer, Micah. Twelve years is a long time, and even I have my limits."

He touched her hair then, grazed his fingertips over her flushed cheek, letting them linger. He could feel her muscles tighten beneath his touch, and suddenly he jerked away, fighting the urge to haul her out of the car and kiss her as he longed to do. Without a backward glance, he strode toward the bank.

The car was hot inside after being locked up in the late May afternoon, but at least it was a haven: A place where she was alone.

After leaving the parking lot Micah turned on the air conditioner and rolled up her window, letting the cool air wash over the sticky wetness of her skin. She wouldn't let herself think about Ian, or money, or how she could gracefully get out of the rental property deal she wanted to buy. And she sure as hell wouldn't think about Chance.

When she reached home, she felt better. In the shadowed solitude surrounding her, she stripped off her damp clothes and threw them onto the big antique tester bed. There were memories there, ones she didn't care to dwell upon. Her guilt lay like a twisted serpent upon the empty mattress. She remembered her aching want of Chance as she had lain in her husband's arms, the fantasies she indulged in even now. It was wrong when she was married, and Jonathon's being dead didn't magically make things right; she still had to live with the memory of her heart's infidelity, the consequences of it.

Micah couldn't stand it, the self-doubt, the whole jumbled mess her life had become. A tepid bath would help, it always did. If nothing else, she could at least escape the salt of sweat still clinging to her body. And if she was lucky, maybe the taint she still felt from Ian's proposition would wash away too.

Usually she wore a robe, even alone. But being as hot as she was, instead walked naked to the adjoining bath. She bent over and adjusted the knobs, making the water cooler than usual, letting the crystal clear wetness wash over her left hand.

The ring was no longer there, and she was glad. If Jonathon hadn't died, it would have been gone by now anyway. She had decided, finally, to leave him just before he had. Somewhere along the line even her pity had run dry, and guilt wasn't a good enough reason to stay.

Staring into the running cascade, Micah let her thoughts wander.

She turned off the faucet, realizing suddenly she needed to conserve on the water bill too. Stepping into the deep, clawfoot tub, Micah shivered from the tepid onslaught against the heat of her skin. She sank down into the liquid tranquility, letting the soothing water wash over her.

Micah tried to look at herself, but as always felt a little self-conscious about her own body. Deliberately she reached for the French-milled soap and lathered her shoulders and breasts. She closed her eyes, and as she swirled the slick lavender bar over her body, eased into the comfort the self-massage rendered.

Just as she thought she'd escaped the worries dogging her every thought, a vision of Chance superimposed itself behind her lids. A heavy sigh escaped. She had treated him badly at the bank, lashing out because he was the first available target. Her predicament wasn't his fault, there was no one to blame but herself. But knowing that didn't diminish her confusion, or the frightening amount of desire she felt for him.

Why, she asked herself, *why are you so afraid of him? Because he's too strong for you, because he can control your emotions, your body? Because you can't bring yourself to trust him, knowing the type of man he's become?*

Yes, yes, and *yes*. All that and more. He'd left her when she was too young to hang on to vague promises about the future.

Micah could feel the constriction of her throat. Back then loosing Chance had seemed like the most terrible thing in the world that could have happened to her.

He'd grown up poor, but was determined not to stay that way. At twenty he took a job in the Gulf working on an oil rig. When he'd left, he told her she didn't understand about things like wanting to do more than survive, to make better than she was born with. He accused her of not being able to imagine eating out of a tin can when she'd been born with a silver spoon in her mouth.

His anger had always been so close to the surface. She remembered that about him, even as a child. She sat upright in the water now, her hair streaming wet down her back. Working in the fragrant shampoo, she pretended she could still feel Chance's hands stroking through the waves as he pressed her against the wall, the way he had tried to soften the blow of reality, of his words.

"You were never meant to know about such things, Micah. It's why I have to leave . . . to get ahead. When I come back here, even your parents will have to accept me."

Her scalp tingled as she washed the suds from her hair, remembering his fingers sliding against her scalp, flexing, pulling her hair into a greedy fist as he rubbed the strands together. She could almost feel the heat of his body against hers, pressing his hips closer until she gasped in genuine shock, in the jolt of her body's answering response.

"Wait for me." His voice so urgent. *"I have dreams and they're always of you. Say you'll wait. Swear it."*

"I do. I swear it, Chance."

"No matter how long I'm gone, no matter who else you see, you'll save yourself for me."

"Yes." She pulled his head down to hers, sealing the vow.

"I'll hold you to that."

And he had held her. His mouth taught her the meaning of pleasure while his hand came up in a smooth motion to cup one of her breasts in his palm, making her shiver beneath him. He was touching her through her clothes, but still she burned. Their bodies strained against each other, undulating in a rhythm that even a virgin understood through the haze of awakening passion, until she cried out with desire, with the fear of it. . . .

"I'm taking you home, Micah. Right now. Before I do something real selfish that we'll both regret."

In the end he had succumbed. But it had been her, not him, who had pushed them past the limit, making the decision that time and fate could never erase. Even now she remembered each minute detail. . . .

The way he had undressed her. The shocking revelation of his nakedness. The supple beauty of restraint as he touched her with such a tender hunger. Even at twenty he had been a skilled lover, gentling her so that there was little pain, and much pleasure. Enough that she could remember the ecstasy of release, the tears he kissed away as he moved within her and murmured endearments she still kept locked tight in her heart.

Micah sighed heavily, reluctant to leave the memory. How she wished she had waited, that Chance had given her some sign throughout the years. For nearly two years she had tried to be patient, and it had been sheer hell, not knowing, wondering if she had imagined his devotion. Or worse, that he had lied to her.

Time had a way of doing that, diluting a person's resolve, transforming memories and promises until they seemed no more than once-upon-a-time dreams. College came and still no word from Chance. Sometime in her freshman year she convinced herself it had all been an adolescent crush.

About that time she met Jonathon. He was handsome and charming, and she thought she might be in love.

She married right out of college. It seemed the practical thing to do. After all, her parents liked him, her friends liked him, and she liked him. It seemed natural, the easy course.

Chance had come back from Lord only knew where a year after her wedding. He wasn't wealthy, but he had done well for himself. When he found her, his lips had formed the word, "Congratulations." But his eyes were accusing.

She thought he would leave, but he didn't. Instead, he seemed determined to make his mark. This time in her own city so she'd be sure to notice. He insinuated himself into the moneyed elite that she had grown up with, flaunting yet another beauty by his side at Mardi Gras balls, social extravaganzas, or in the society pages. Whenever they saw each other, there was always an uneasy tension between them. But their secret remained just that.

And so here she was, wanting him more than ever. And more than ever he was past her reach.

Dear Lord, how she wanted him. Even knowing

his reputation for cruelty, she ached to have him hold her again.

For so long that was all she ever wanted. But it just wasn't enough anymore. Something else called to her, demanding to be satisfied. It came from deep inside—this growing need to prove she could be strong, that she could survive all on her own. And what was so strange was that of all the people she knew, the one person who would truly understand was Chance.

So the cards were at long last on the table. For a terrifying moment she felt the old weakness threaten. She wobbled like a newborn colt, then found her footing still good.

Micah smiled as she claimed the small victory. She was going to make a new life for herself, starting today. But above all else, she swore two things:

She would fight.

She would win.

Three

The phone rang and Micah reached down to pick it up. She stopped just before touching it, in a moment of debate. Tentatively she touched the receiver on the fourth ring.

"Hello?" Her voice was as breathy as if she had been running.

"Micah? Hi. It's Elliot."

"Elliot?" she echoed, hoping her voice didn't reveal her disappointment.

"What do you mean, 'Elliot?' If I didn't know better, I'd think you were disappointed to hear from me." He laughed at his joke.

Micah forced a faint laugh. "Of course not, Elliot. That's nonsense. How've you been?"

"I'm not sure. A lot depends on what kind of reaction I get from you."

That was Elliot Sebastian for you, Micah mused. Good for a laugh, and good with a line. But over-all he was a pretty decent kind of guy as long as you didn't expect much depth.

"What kind of reaction were you looking for?"

Micah could feel herself blush, embarrassed by the almost flirtatious comeback.

"Sounds like you're doing just fine, Micah. I was afraid to call sooner. I mean, I didn't want to—"

"That's okay, Elliot, I know what you mean. And I appreciate your concern."

"Would that extend to going out with me this Sunday? I don't want to rush you or anything, but I thought . . . Well, the way things were, I figured you might be ready to get out by now."

So, Micah thought, Elliot knew too. It seemed everyone knew she had little to regret.

"Micah?" Elliot said into the silence. "I'd like to take you to the opera. That is if you're up to it."

She should say something, do something. Anything but stand there dumbly with the receiver in her hand. This was so unexpected.

"Yes," she said quickly before she could change her mind. "I'd like to get out, Elliot . . . Sunday night at seven o'clock? . . . Of course . . . Yes, I'll look forward to it too."

Micah hung up after the date was made, wondering what in the world had gotten into her. She wasn't any more interested in Elliot than a rerun of a bad dream.

Why had she agreed then . . . why? The answer was too obvious. She was lashing out at Chance for not pursuing her further, disappointment propelling her to make a date she couldn't even look forward to. So what did that make her? She was using Elliot to get back at Chance. It was a cheap shot and totally unworthy of her. Micah reached for the telephone, ready to call him back and cancel.

A vision of her spare cupboard and the few cartons of yogurt in the refrigerator caused her stomach to growl. And how long had it been since she'd been out? The women she had mistook for friends in the old social arena had turned out to be about as genuine as fool's gold.

Micah hesitated, then moved away from the phone, trying to feel better about her decision. Her motives weren't right, but she'd make it up to him. She would make sure Elliot enjoyed the date whether she did or not.

"Micah? Aren't you enjoying this?" Elliot whispered to her behind his program, and Micah realized she was staring off, away from the stage.

"Yes, fine," she whispered back, and made herself smile.

Elliot nodded, seemingly satisfied, and went back to watching the opera. Micah kept her eyes on the action even though her mind continued to wander.

At intermission she was relieved to have the excuse to escape to the ladies' room. Elliot seemed in need of constant conversation, and it was just a little more than she was up to right now.

Serves you right, her conscience taunted. Yogurt might not be chateaubriand, but at least she could keep her self-esteem while she ate it in the hot, muggy house. Just thinking about the heat waiting at home made her feel a surge of appreciation for the cool jets of air flowing around the rest room.

Micah touched up her makeup, then glanced at her reflection in the full-length mirror. Her dress was elegantly simple—a strapless white silk. It plunged so that her throat was left bare to reveal the necklace of a single emerald nestled in the hollow there, setting off the brilliant luster of matching stones which dropped in gold filigree from her ears.

The set was her grandmother's. She really should have sold it along with the rest of her jewelry, but when the jeweler started to reach for the set, she had instinctively covered them with her hand, and told him they were no longer for sale.

Although she was tempted to stay rooted in the ladies' room for the duration of the evening, good manners dictated that she go find Elliot at their appointed meeting place—beside the champagne table. She shut the clasp to her gold-beaded bag, gritted her teeth, and left.

Micah decided he must have been watching for her, and tried to ignore the twinge of irritation when he gestured from the distance, champagne glass in hand. The smile she wore was vague, and she was glad she didn't have to meet his eyes as she wove her way through the mass of people. When he was only a few feet away, she realized her mistake.

"Look who's here, Micah. We were waiting for you."

The limp feeling she had been fighting throughout the evening surged into an explosion of anticipation, of apprehension. Something like a light went on inside her head, and she felt simultaneously giddy and bereft.

It was the gorgeous blonde draped on Chance's arm that caused her heart to drop flat. Micah had thought she looked alluring, but she felt dull in this woman's radiant shadow.

"I'm glad to see you're out of mourning, Micah. White suits you a lot better than black." Chance smiled politely, then reached for her hand and pressed a light kiss to it. With a shock she felt his tongue flick over her skin. He did it so discreetly, so skillfully, no one else seemed to notice what he'd done.

He let go and turned back to his date, and made the polite introductions. Micah realized with a start she was standing there with her mouth dropped open and quickly closed it.

Elliot said something, and she nodded, without even hearing a word he'd said. How could Chance have done it so easily—scaled her protective wall before she could erect a single defense? She felt stunned, rendered helpless to her need for him, the need that had been growing since she had come to realize it was only her keeping them apart now.

Elliot cleared his throat. "The curtain must be about to open. They're flicking the lights. Shall we go, Micah?"

Mutely she nodded as Elliot nudged her toward the door. With an unprecedented surge of jealousy Micah watched as the other woman clung to Chance's arm. He slipped Micah a satisfied smile, and she knew he was pleased by her own artless reaction. Then he fit his arm snugly about the woman's waist and pulled her closer. The coup de grace left Micah feeling wounded. She couldn't have hurt more if someone had driven a knife between her ribs.

He raised a single dark brow in her direction, and the silent message he sent was clear. *Come to me, Micah. Come to me soon. If you don't, someone else gladly will.*

Micah could feel herself flush with the stinging heat suffusing her cheeks. How adept he was at the game. How ingenuous she must appear in comparison.

And wasn't she?

The whole episode was a biting reminder of just how out of her league he was. That woman he was with suited him. She was probably a model, or a professional of some sort. And what was she? A twenty-eight-year-old woman who couldn't get a job, had managed to screw up her life despite all her childhood advantages, and was just now starting to "find herself." The comparison was disgusting.

By the time she took her seat again in the theater, Micah was miserable. But somewhere from the far reaches a tiny voice emerged, refusing to be shut down. It insisted that she would learn, that she was a good person who deserved a good life. She must not give up.

The voice was faint, but it sufficed. She squared her shoulders and mustered a slight smile, determined to salvage the evening with as much grace as she could.

The smile didn't reach her eyes. But Elliot smiled back and she knew it was enough.

* * *

"Well, good night, Elliot. Thank you for a lovely evening."

Micah extended her hand and Elliot hesitated, then took it and squeezed. He bent forward and kissed her lightly on the lips.

It felt strange to have another man touch her. She didn't find it unpleasant, but it wasn't overly exciting either. It was just . . . strange, unfamiliar.

She was glad he didn't try to linger or deepen the kiss as she pulled away. Micah smiled and said "Good night" once more, then turned to unlock her front door. As she twisted the key she felt Elliot's hand come over hers.

"Wait, Micah. I want to talk with you about something." Elliot kept his voice low, almost intimate.

It was all she could do not to groan aloud.

"Elliot," she said firmly, "I'm not interested in continuing the evening."

Elliot coughed and looked slightly embarrassed as he glanced away.

"It's not exactly that." He paused then went on, looking at her uneasily. "I have an IOU, Micah. Jonathon's signature is on it. If you can, I need you to make good on his debt." He hesitated, then added, "It's for five thousand dollars."

Micah was stunned. He wasn't interested in her, he just wanted his money!

"Money?" she asked on a short, incredulous laugh. "I'm sorry, Elliot, you didn't beat the crowd. People had to take a number to get their cut. I didn't realize half the population of New

Orleans played poker with my late husband until the day after he died."

Elliot looked down to the ground, then up again, his eyes skittering uneasily away from hers.

"When can you pay it then?"

Micah could feel the gathering rise of her temper. She couldn't seem to get away from the ever-present worry about money no matter what. Her instincts took over, and she struck back in self-defense.

"When I have it and not before," she said through clenched teeth. "Now leave, Elliot. And don't call me again. We might not have had much to talk about before, but we have nothing to discuss after tonight."

She stared him down, and it was with a delicious sense of triumph that Micah watched him walk away until he got into his car and drove off.

Her face felt unnaturally tight, and her raw nerves seemed dangerously close to snapping now that she was alone and could lower her guard.

Pressing her forehead against the dark wood, she fought the urge to slump into a heap on the porch and sob her misery aloud. Micah drew a deep, shaky breath as she bent to twist the key in the bronzed lock, and it was then she heard the footsteps. They were heavy and deliberate as they came closer. She looked up and her heart stopped in midbeat.

Four

Chance had been waiting for a good twenty minutes before he heard the car pull up in Micah's driveway. He was leaning against the side of the veranda, away from their sight, but positioned so that he could see a thin strip of the couple walking hand in hand up the steps to the front door.

His own hands curled tight around the wood supporting him, so tight he could feel a splinter digging its way beneath the skin of a finger. He knew it was wrong, but he couldn't stop himself from listening and watching.

Chance tried to decipher just what it was he was feeling as he watched their brief kiss. Hard as he wanted to believe he had evolved beyond jealousy or making his point with a fist, in that moment he knew it was a lie.

All the old emotions roiled inside of him, the baseness of rage and possessiveness. He might have done a good job of polishing his image, but the man on the inside hadn't changed much.

Micah was his one weakness. Despite his wealth and power, he still felt something lacking. She was the one thing he'd wanted and never had. Watching Micah with Elliot now only steeled his resolve to win her back, never to let another man touch her again. She belonged to him body and soul, and he was going to make damn sure she realized it.

Their kiss ended quickly and Chance loosened his grip upon the railing. His mouth settled into a satisfied smile as he saw her turn back to the door, obviously putting an early end to the night.

Then he saw Elliot restraining her hand, and his slight smile faded while he fought the impulse to bound out of the shadows and thrust him away. When Elliot began speaking to her again, Chance leaned forward, straining to hear.

What he heard brought a mixed reaction. He wasn't surprised, of course. Jonathon had owed a lot of money to a lot of people.

But now it seemed Elliot was hassling her. Chance almost gave himself away, by stepping in to tell the guy to shove off when Micah turned on him. Chance was proud of the way she stood up for herself, seeing a building strength.

Elliot turned away, leaving quickly. And then he was gone. Even from the distance Chance could see the strain in her features, the hollowness of her cheekbones accentuated by the shadows of dark chasing across her face.

Micah. How many years had that name haunted him? Asleep, awake, even when he tried to blot it out of his mind in a thousand different ways, with a host of different women. He had a secret, a very private one. Each woman in the dark had become Micah in that fleeting moment of release. The act may have started with someone else, but in his mind it always ended with her.

And there she was, so close he could speak and she would hear him in the near silence of night sounds. She twisted the key, and his legs moved of their own volition, taking several steps away from the darkness and into the shadow of half-light.

"I've been waiting."

Micah jerked as though startled by the sound of his voice. She turned quickly to face him, and Chance could feel his heart tighten, his loins quicken. *Damn her* that she should have that kind of hold over him.

"Chance," she whispered and stepped back as he came closer.

He hated seeing the wariness creep across her face.

"Why are you here?" she rushed on suddenly as he walked deliberately toward her.

"Why?" he asked, still walking until he stopped less than an arm's length away. "What do *you* think? Go ahead, Micah, go ahead and say it. Tell me why I'm here."

Chance could see the changes click in one by one. The way she began to breathe faster, the wariness in her eyes changing to a darker shade of emerald, as though she were responding already against her will.

"We both know why you're here," she finally

said. "And it's impossible." She took a protective step back toward the door.

"Stop it," he commanded. "Just stop what you're doing *right now*." His voice came out harsher than he meant it to as he gripped her wrist and pulled her toward him.

Micah did stop. She went very still. Only her face was animated, and it was the fear in it that goaded Chance to smash the defenses she was throwing up faster than he could hurdle them.

He let her wrist go only to lay his hands over the soft ripple of muscle beneath her upper arms.

"Quit running from me, Micah. Quit running from yourself. That's the coward's way out, *ma cher*. You said you wanted to stand on your own two feet. Well, go ahead. Do it. Prove to us both that you're tough, brave. Face the truth for once, the truth about us. Cards on the table, Micah. The stakes are high, so take your best shot."

Micah flinched at the analogy, and Chance cursed softly under his breath for not choosing better.

She seemed to steady herself then, something coming into her eyes he hadn't seen before—the same something he had heard in her voice when she'd told Elliot where he could take it. A certain self-possession and determination.

"All right," she said, her voice coming out stronger than before.

"You scare me, Chance," she blurted out suddenly. "The way you're touching me scares me. I don't like where I've been. I'm not sure where I'm going. All I know is, you're dangerous and you have cause to resent me. You want the truth? All right you've got it. You've hurt me before, Chance, and maybe I've even done the same to you. Only I'm not willing to take the risk of it happening again. So let me be. If you care for me, you'll do that."

Chance hesitated, wanting her, needing her. He couldn't back off, especially not now.

"I care for you," he murmured in an even tone. "Enough that I want to help. Give me a chance to prove it, Micah. Don't I deserve that much?" He waited for an answer, but she stayed quiet. "Or am I so vile you're not even willing to give me that? Still the bad boy of New Orleans trying to corrupt the most innocent little rich girl in the parish?"

"No," she said quickly.

"No?" he repeated with obvious disbelief.

"It was always *you*, Chance. You made sure I didn't forget the differences between us when we were growing up. And maybe the differences are even greater now that you've established yourself. I'm still unfashionably 'wholesome' as you once put it. But I've *never* treated you as though you weren't good enough. So don't try to push that off on me."

"You're right," he said reluctantly. "I admit that wasn't fair."

"Then can you admit you still resent me? I still feel it sometimes, Chance. Not as much as when you first came back, but I sense it's still there."

He nodded. "Let's talk about it, Micah. About us. Where we went wrong, what's keeping us apart. Talk to me. Don't be afraid of me anymore . . . Please."

He must have gotten through to her somehow,

because Micah swayed toward him and he drew her closer, almost against his chest, but not quite. She didn't try to move away and he gave a silent shout of joy. It had been too long in coming. He wanted to see her face, to feel her breasts barely touching him through the open dinner jacket. The lightness of the contact was more exciting than crushing her body to his. He moved so that there was a slight friction, and he could feel her response, the tightening of her nipples as they thrust against his tailored white shirt.

With all the will he possessed he made himself stop. He wasn't a randy kid anymore. He wasn't about to blow what little ground they had gained by acting like one.

"Do I matter to you, Chance?" she asked quietly. "Sometimes I could almost believe that. Lord knows I've wanted to often enough. But it's not that easy with us. We have a past. One that's laced with resentment from you."

"You have none?"

"No. I've escaped that, but not the guilt."

Slowly he nodded. Wordlessly he led her to the porch steps, and wordlessly she followed. They sat down in the dark in silence while a distant car sped in the background, overridden by the concert of crickets.

Chance reached for her hand.

"I'll try not to resent you," he said quietly. She shifted, and he could feel her looking at him now. Into the gathering darkness he stared, struggling to pry open the wall of indifference he'd kept firmly in place too long to easily put aside.

"I know it wasn't your fault," he went on. "You were too young. I asked too much. I *know* all that, and I've told myself those very words in silence, and just as often aloud. But it doesn't seem to make any difference. I find that I do resent you every now and then. But Micah," he turned to look at her, his gaze intense, "It's not that you didn't wait for me, I didn't blame you for that. Maybe at first, but that soon faded. It's not even that you had all the advantages I didn't growing up. I admit there's anger there. But it's never been aimed at you."

"Then what is it, Chance? What *do* you hold against me if not that?"

He shook his head, amazed that she could overlook something so obvious. He loosened her hand in a gesture of contrasting gentleness and held it palm up, tracing the crevices, the soft inner pads beneath his fingertips. He thrilled to the way she shivered against him in spite of the warm air surrounding them.

"Don't you know? It's that you kept the distance when you had no right to. I left you alone as long as you were happy. I figured the fault was mine for not coming back sooner, not keeping some kind of contact over the years. But when I could see your marriage crumbling, the misery you were living in, while I was just as miserable— in another way—" He stopped and for a moment remembered . . . the empty nights, the ever-present longing she had created only to leave him with it alone, with no hope, no surcease.

"Chance," she said, breaking into his thoughts, "That was the point. I was married."

"You called *that* a marriage?"

Micah winced, and her eyes appeared unnaturally bright.

"I'm doing it again. Dammit, I don't mean to, Micah. I was never a gentle man, it's just not in me. But when I see you, when I touch you—" He laid his fingertips lightly against her cheek and was amazed to see that she shook. Chance exhaled a long stream of breath. "I'm a hard man if ever there was one . . . but lady, you turn me inside out. And when you get right down to it, that's why I resent you. I resent you for not leaving him when I asked you to, but more than that, I resent the hell out of you for jerking my emotions around like a puppet on a string."

Her heart was racing. "I never meant to," she whispered. "You know I never did."

"Yeah, I do. And that's the point. You do it without even meaning to. You think I'm dangerous, Micah? Think again, because it works both ways."

Chance could see her swallow hard, the tapered length of her neck straining so that he wanted to trail his lips against the purity of her skin until he felt her murmurs of arousal vibrate beneath his mouth. He forced his eyes back to hers and knew she believed him. He was ceding power by betraying his emotions. But he was gambling that she would feel safer with that knowledge, safe enough to take a step closer, to begin bridging the gap.

"It wouldn't have been right," she said, her voice low. "He was a sick man, Chance. When you brought him home that night two years ago, I wanted to. More than anything I wanted to leave with you and never . . . ," her voice caught for a moment. "It took everything I had in me to stay, to do what was right."

"Turning your back on us wasn't right. Staying because of a sense of duty wasn't right. You didn't love him, Micah. Admit it."

"No." There, she'd said it, but she knew it wouldn't satisfy him. "Chance, I have to look at this face in the mirror every morning. If I had left him for you, I couldn't have lived with it. My self-respect, everything I'd ever been taught about loyalty, marriage—"

Chance placed a finger over her lips, halting the flow of words. The physical contact sent a rush through him and he forgot about everything except the smooth, full texture of her lips, the feel of her ripe plum-colored lipstick rubbing against his thumb.

"I kissed you that night. Do you remember?" he whispered.

Micah nodded, her eyes deep, unfathomable pools of remembrance. As she spoke he traced the movement of her lips.

"I remember. While he slept, passed out, you came to me. You held me. Kissed me."

"You kissed me back as hard and deep as that night when we were just kids. I wanted you, Micah. Right then, in the same room with him. Nothing would have made me happier than for that sorry bastard to have woken up and found you in my arms. He would have let you go then. As a matter of honor, if nothing else. He had that much gumption—little more, but that much."

"I was married," she whispered again. "Leaving like that . . . Chance, it wouldn't have been right."

"No," he agreed. "Not for you. Not for my Micah. You made me leave, and even then you clung to your guilt, didn't you? You pushed me further away than ever."

"I had to. I *still* have to." She suddenly buried her face in her hands and drew a shuddering breath. "Oh, Chance. So much has happened, so much I wish I could undo. I'm a different person now, and I have to live with that fact. We can't pick up where we left off. That isn't how life works."

Chance's brow furrowed. *"Why?"* he said between gritted teeth. "You keep harboring your secrets like they're sacred sins. Why, Micah? Do you think it's some kind of saintly accomplishment that you can cling to, or is it some kind of ridiculous loyalty to a dead man who didn't even deserve it while he was alive?"

"No," she said fiercely. "This time it's for *me*. Can't you understand, Chance? You're too strong, too overpowering. For the first time I have the chance to have a life of my own. I have to prove to myself I can *be* somebody, *all on my own*. You said as much to me so long ago. Well, maybe I didn't understand then. But I understand now. Can't you do the same?"

She suddenly leaned forward and dug her fingers into his shoulders, her face set in fervent lines, as though the truth were even now just emerging for her.

"Please, Chance. You say you care. If you do,

then let me go. Then maybe I'll find what I'm looking for. Can't you just be my friend?"

It was the last question that truly touched him. Micah was right. He couldn't force her, but maybe there was a way to win the new Micah. There had to be a way.

"Okay, Micah," he said. "Unfortunately, I understand. Only tell me one thing. What's your plan?"

"My plan?"

"Of course. How do you propose to go about this 'evolvement' of yours?"

Micah seemed puzzled, as though she had been trying to find the path and was stumbling blindly in search of it. Then her brow smoothed and her eyes lit up.

"You said you were always there if I needed you. I need your advice, Chance. You're the only one I can turn to for this. Will you help me?"

"What d'you mean asking me a question like that? Of course I'll help you. Anything, Micah. Is it money? I heard Elliot, and I can take care of him. Anyone else who's giving you a hard time?"

"Absolutely not!"

He was stunned by the vehemence in her voice. "I don't want your money, Chance. I only want what I can earn for myself. As for Elliot, and anyone like him, they can wait until I've got it to give. Whatever you do, don't offer me money again. *Ever.*"

Chance shrugged. He didn't understand; nothing would make him happier than lightening her financial load. But if that's the way she wanted it . . . well, he'd let her call the shots. For now.

"Okay, we'll leave the money out of it. So tell me what you need."

Micah smiled then, really smiled for the first time since he could remember. She was always beautiful, but when she smiled she was something else.

"Oh, you have it, all right. I've got a little over three thousand dollars to my name, Chance. It's my money, some I tucked away. I can't get a job so I thought I might start a business. Something of my own that I can take pride in, make enough at to support myself. You had to start somewhere, learn all the ropes. I can't afford to make many mistakes. You can help me steer clear of the more fatal ones. You could tell me where to invest what I've got." He started to comment, but she rushed on to finish.

"Now, don't suggest the antique business—I might have the knowledge, but after going bankrupt, my reputation is shot. Even if it wasn't my fault. Besides, my family was interested in hunting down old pieces and selling them. I'm not."

Chance thought about it for a few minutes. It wasn't a question of helping her, that didn't even enter his mind. The real question was, how to help her and implicate her into his life at the same time?

"A little over three thousand dollars, huh?"

Micah leaned forward, anxious. "I know it's not much, but—"

"No," he said quickly. "It's enough. I already have a working idea. I want to sleep on it, though." He looked at Micah's eager face. There was a youthful zest there he hadn't seen in a very,

very long while. "Can you meet me at my office tomorrow? Say ten o'clock?"

Micah nodded with barely leashed excitement, and Chance could feel his own delight. Although he made all the usual charitable donations, he hadn't really helped many people before. The rush of pleasure he received from helping her felt good. But then again, he wasn't doing this totally out of the goodness of his hard heart. It was all part of his plan to make her his. All his.

"I'll be there," she promised. "Ten o'clock sharp. But you have to promise me, Chance, no dirty dealings, and no preferential treatment. I want you to treat me like you would any other person looking for advice about an investment."

Chance held back a laugh. "You know me better than that, Micah. I wouldn't give most people the time of day if they came to me with the same question. Don't give me too much credit—underneath it all, I'm still a street-tough kid. I'll get my money's worth even if I do still have it bad for a sweet young girl." He was trying to tease her, but he saw her draw back. Quickly he added, "Don't worry. No special treatment. We'll keep it strictly business."

He forced himself to rise before he sealed the lie with a kiss. He knew she would trust him more if he ended the night now, and he wasn't going to test his luck. He was pleased that she seemed to hesitate, disappointed that he was leaving so quickly.

He reached for her hand, helping her up then walking her to the door.

Chance skimmed his fingertips across the delicate ridge of her jaw until he touched the emerald dangling at one of her lobes. He raised it up, ever so slightly, until it glittered in the moonlight. Her breathing quickened, and the way she looked at him . . . he suddenly ached with the familiar swelling of his groin, the tightening around his heart.

"What I did at the opera, Micah. It was . . . unkind. I was jealous about seeing you with Elliot, and . . . I'm sorry." He knew he'd hurt her, but she accepted his apology easily, gracing him with a smile.

"You looked so beautiful tonight," he said in a thick, slumberous voice. "I saw you weaving your way over to us, before you knew I was there. I could see these earrings swaying as you walked, the way they matched your eyes. More than anything I wanted to go to you, to kiss you right there, to touch these stones that were as close as I wanted to be. Do you ever want me half as much, Micah? Do you ever remember our kisses, our lovemaking, and relive it all over again? I do. I've replayed them in my mind until they're as much a part of me as breathing. I only wish I knew that you felt the same way. That's all I ask for now, nothing more. Tell me if you still want me, and I promise to leave it at that."

She was yielding to his words. She turned her cheek until her lips were nestled in his palm. She kissed his hand.

"I do, Chance," she said fervently. "I want you more than I've ever wanted any other man. I've cried at night from wanting you so much."

He took the gamble and laid it on the line.

"Then want me more. If I so much as kiss you again, it'll be only when you ask for it. Not before. You've cut your space and, heaven help me, I'm going to give it. When you're ready, Micah, I'll be waiting."

Chance covered her hand with his own, shutting his eyes against the intensity of what he was feeling.

He drew her into his embrace, and for the space of a few moments—moments that passed too damnably fast—he trusted himself to hold her. She laid her head against his chest and he cradled her there, stroking through her hair until he encountered the clasp that burrowed at the nape of her neck. He touched the clasp, wanting fiercely to release it, to plunge his hands into the silken strands which were as black as the night surrounding them. But he didn't dare. He made himself take a step back, releasing her, letting her go.

"Good night," he murmured. Quickly he turned and took two steps. For a moment he thought he must have imagined her next words, but he paused and waited for her to speak again.

"Chance," she whispered, "kiss me?"

Five

Micah heard her own words echo between her ears. What was she thinking, giving into the gathering tide of emotion, of physical awareness that was too acute, almost painful—asking for pain of a different kind?

But she had said it, those words she had been fighting against all night, and now even with her eyes closed, she could hear him retracing his steps, slowly coming closer. Over the heavy rushing beat of her heart, she knew he was pacing himself, deliberately slow, increasing her anticipation with the thud of his weight upon the groaning wood of the porch.

And then he stopped. Chance didn't touch her, but she could hear the slight husk of his breath, feel the heat emanate in waves off his body and lap at hers. Her nostrils dilated at the familiar, masculine musk scent that brought the years crashing back. Her palms were damp, her legs were trembling. She didn't dare to open her eyes and meet his. Because even in the muted darkness enveloping them, she could feel the pull and weight of their hold.

"Not like this, Micah." He touched her cheek so tenderly she felt the impulse to cry.

She opened her eyes and met his. They were the color of coal and just as indecipherable.

"Then, like what, Chance? Tell me." It was all she could do to force the words past the constriction of desire too heavy in her throat. Silently she added, *anything, just tell me. Just kiss me.*

"Like . . . this." His lips were open, parted, closing the distance to hers. But he didn't join their mouths. Rather, he caught her hand, dangling limply by her side, and kissed the center of her palm before draping it about his neck. She could feel the corded, dark strength beneath her fingertips, the texture of thick hair, and the stiff white collar of his shirt intruding over the skin she longed to touch.

"Your hands are shaking, Micah," he murmured. "And they're damp. Do you have any idea how that makes me feel? Knowing I can still do that to you after all these years?"

She shook her head, and stroked her fingers tentatively through the ebony thickness, then with a surer touch.

Chance's breath came out in a single, heavy stream as she continued to seek her fill of his scent and texture and nearness.

"It makes me feel . . . incredible. Invincible. Like every minute I've waited was worth it. Look, Micah—" he held his hand up close to her face. "See what you do to me? You're the only woman who's ever made *me* tremble. And inside it's the same. I hate it. I love it. And nothing, not time, not distance, nothing's been able to dull the memories. It's been the same for you, I know it has. But I want to hear you say it. Tell me what it does to you when I touch your hair like this—"

He reached around and suddenly she could feel the weight of her hair loosened, falling around her shoulders, spilling between his fingers. "Or when I hold you to me like this—" the same fingers speared through to the roots and tightened as his other arm came around and soothed a trail over her spine before locking around her waist. *"Tell me."*

She swallowed hard, trying to deal with the tumult of sensation, the difficulty of putting it into words. She'd always felt this way with Chance, but she had never spoken it aloud, never dared. What he wanted was difficult. And once said, she couldn't take it back. Oh yes, he knew what he was doing, the words he demanded. Only she couldn't seem to draw back, to cling to reason while he stood so close, withholding himself, denying her what she craved.

"Chance, I . . ." His hands tightened in her hair, around her waist. His mouth lowered until his breath mingled with hers. She instinctively pulled him closer.

"That's a start. You what, Micah? Need me?"

"Yes," she whispered.

"And what else?"

"I . . . I want you."

"Badly?"

She nodded.

"How bad, Micah? Enough to let go of what's holding you back from telling me what I want to hear?"

She took a shuddering breath. "It's hard for me, Chance. I've never talked about these things before."

"Then it's time you did. Just trust me for once, tell me what I make you feel . . . here, I'll even help you—" He passed his hand from her hair to press his fingertips against the vein pounding beside her neck. "Does your heart beat too fast?"

A tiny moan broke past her lips as he stroked his fingertips over the length of her throat. Too familiar. Too wonderfully seductive.

"Yes, you know it does. Just as you know I can't think—good Lord, I can hardly breathe. And it's torture. The kind I could die for. *There.* Are you happy? Is that what you want me to say, to admit?" Something held her back from saying more, though, a sense of self-preservation, the possible cost of saying too much.

"There," she said again, this time softly. "Is that enough for you, Chance? I hope so, because tonight that's as much as I can give. And it's a lot more than I intended at that."

"It's enough." His voice was gruff and deep with longing. "For now it's enough."

His mouth fell upon hers, swift and hot and wanting. Not the kiss of curiosity, of lips touching for the first time. It was a kiss of reunion, of knowing the hidden secrets that bound them, the parlay of tongues meeting in desire that had been kept in check too long.

Micah felt no hesitancy, only elation, ecstasy that his mouth moved over hers with such hungry abandon. The stroke of his tongue over hers before tracing the shape of her teeth, her lips. The command he demanded and she gave.

His mouth was open, skimming from her lips to her neck, her ear. Micah pressed eagerly against him and felt the wonderful proof of his maleness, the intoxicating rush of knowing she did this to him, that the power was mutual and equally as strong.

She wrapped her arm more tightly about his neck, treading her fingers through the resilient thickness of his hair, hungry for the feel of it. Her other arm she tightened around his waist, pulling him closer still, heedless of what she might be doing to him. Wanting to test the feeling. Delighting to those sounds again, harsh and guttural sounds of unrestrained longing. To know that in spite of the years, in spite of her self-doubts, she could still make his blood pound through his veins as he did hers.

The warm spring air hit the wetness on her neck, the delicious, smooth trail he forged until mindlessly she moaned against his tiny bites, her head dropping back to invite more. The feel of his teeth skimming her jaw while his hands tangled in her hair was everything that she remembered, everything and more.

"Chance . . . please. More . . ." She moved until her lips found his again. They felt full and a little raw. The ravaging was too delicious, too wonderful for words. And she needed it yet again. Enough to make up for all the lonely nights she had dreamed of this moment, this little portion of what she truly craved.

Chance's hands began to slide down her back, but stopped just short of her buttocks. And the disappointment—oh the heaviness of it—of his not touching her more intimately, the frustration of not being able to make herself say "Please, touch me there. Run your hands down my back until they can go no farther. Then trail them over my skin, beneath my dress. Touch me until I don't care anymore." Be brave, she told herself. Be brave, be foolish. Give in to what you would never dare before. . . .

No.

She didn't dare. This time the price was too high.

"I'm waiting, Micah. If you want more than kisses . . . you have to ask for that too. Each . . . and every . . . thing."

She wanted him. She burned for his touch.

Quickly, before she lost what pitifully little control she'd gained, she loosened her hold around his waist and laid her hand full against his chest, not pushing him away, not wanting to, but keeping the slight distance. It was an inner battle not to clench the fabric tight and gather him to her instead.

"No, Chance," she said huskily, shakily. "I don't think so. We'd better stop here."

He drew back and straightened. "Like I said, Micah. I won't push." He touched her cheek gently, the gesture tender, familiar. His face softened in such a way she wanted to kiss him even more than before, to hold that rare show of vulnerability to her and never let go.

"I know what I am," he said, "and so do you. Maybe that tells you how much I care. Because in spite of every instinct screaming inside me to take what I want, knowing you wouldn't say no if I pressed just the right buttons, it would just be for now. Now's not enough. It never has been. I'm going to have you, Micah, and your body's just part of what I need. I'll do whatever it takes." He placed a soft, lingering kiss on her forehead and stepped back. "Whatever it takes," he repeated.

Micah could feel the melting in her, the way her heart shifted at the strength, the honest need he didn't try to hide. His openness disarmed her in a way force never would have.

Chance unlocked the door and pushed it open. He looked for a moment into the entry.

"It's been a long time, hasn't it?" he said, almost to himself.

"Yes, it has, Chance."

"Remember when I knocked on the door that night, and your father answered?"

Micah shivered. How well she remembered indeed.

"I'll never forget him telling me you weren't there, and I could see you looking down from the top of the stairs. I could even see the anger on your face, fighting with the tears. But still you didn't come down."

She swallowed on the sense of impotence she felt then, the disappointment in herself for not being brave enough to face down her father.

"I was afraid to. I knew my father would make a scene if I did."

Chance nodded. "Yeah, that's exactly what would have happened. Looking back now though, I probably would have done the same thing if it had been my daughter. Only I didn't see it that way then, especially when he reminded me about my reputation and how he screened your dates. The way he blocked my way with his arm propped against the frame, I got the message just fine. He wasn't about to let me through that front door for all the tea in China. When I left for good, that was the image I took with me—because when I came back, I was determined to have enough clout that he wouldn't dare block my way again. My mother might have used the back door, but I was damned if I was going to."

It came back at her. Her frustration at her parents. Chance's bitterness about the way her parents treated him, about his mother's role as housekeeper in their household . . .

"I hurt for you, Chance. If only I could have been with you when it happened. If I could have helped or—"

"You helped. You came to her funeral. It helped . . . seeing you there."

"She was a good person, Chance. My parents . . . I . . . well, we appreciated all her . . ."

"That's okay, Micah. You can say it," he had said sadly. " 'All her help.' Let's face it, she was your maid. As much as I hate what her life was, denying it won't change a damn thing. Besides, when I start to feel the anger I

*always remind myself that at least it brought
me to you.*"

"Micah? Are you still with me?"

She started. For a moment it had seemed so
real, she could still feel the rage within him, the
anguish of his mother's loss he had shared with
no one but her.

She smiled, relieved to be standing in the
present.

"I'm with you. I was just thinking that,
maybe—"

"Maybe?" he prompted.

She let him see the hope, the warmth he had
brought to the surface. If he could trust enough
to open up, maybe it was time she found the
courage to do the same.

"Maybe I could fix dinner one night . . . but
you'd have to come through the front door."

He smiled broadly, and it gave him an almost
boyish appearance.

"Dinner one night? Why, Miss Micah, I'd be
delighted." He touched the earring once and then
let it fall. "And you know, I've always preferred
the front door to the back."

They laughed quietly together in the faded
glow of the entry light spilling out and over
them. And then they fell silent with the small
distance between them, the mutual desire still
humming.

"Good night, Chance," she said, reluctantly
stepping over the threshold and into the light.

"Yeah, you too . . . *ma cherie.*" Chance leaned
forward as though he meant to kiss her again,

but almost instantly he pulled away and took a single step back.

"Tomorrow, then?"

Micah nodded and smiled tentatively, not quite able to reorient herself to the sudden change. Not really wanting to.

"Ten o'clock. I'll be there."

Six

At ten minutes of ten Micah stood in the outer waiting area to Chance's office, her hair down and the emerald earrings dangling beside the dark tresses. She nervously glanced into a mirror hanging over a plush couch across from the secretary's empty desk.

She had agonized over what to wear, wondered if Chance would notice the earrings or the hair, and hoped he'd had as much trouble sleeping as she had. The mirror told her the concealer had done a decent job of hiding the circles beneath her eyes.

Her stomach churned with the knowledge Chance was on the other side of the door. The lobby she was waiting in was starkly beautiful, obviously professionally decorated. She'd always known where Chance had his offices, she'd even driven past several times on the pretext of going somewhere else; but she'd never been inside until now.

The secretary had apparently stepped out for a few minutes, and rather than fidget alone, she decided to go ahead and confront Chance.

Tapping lightly on the heavy door, she waited for Chance to open it, or at least to say "Come in."

No sound. Maybe if she just cracked it ajar to call out to let him know she was here . . .

"—I don't give a damn what it takes! Just hang him. No, I don't want him fired! I want him worse than fired—demoted until he's back where he started—"

There was a small silence while Chance stood with his back to her, facing the wall of windows which magnificently displayed the dark sheen of the Mississippi River.

She knew she should move away, go back to the outer office, but the vindictive chill of his voice seemed to pin her where she stood. Cold fingers of warning wrapped themselves around her heart, telling her to stay away from *this* Chance, the one who was heartless and cruel. The one that made her want to cry because he defamed a part of himself, the part that made her weak with longing.

He cursed into the receiver again. "Then what's taking so long? You've had a month—"

Micah swallowed hard as he swung around abruptly. His eyes were flat, biting hard for that split second before he saw her. And then they changed: Sudden delight, then realization that she had heard—wariness now as she stood with her eyes wide, a stricken look on her face she couldn't hide away before he saw it.

"I'll get back to you on this."

He hung up without saying "good-bye," and for a moment they stood watching each other.

Chance raked a hand through his thick, dark hair, mussing it so that he looked even more inviting. Micah tried to disregard it. Just as she tried to disregard the way his sleeves were rolled up, revealing the masculine appeal of hair covering his forearms, the tops of his hands. A man's hands that were large, well formed, and looked as though they had done years of hard labor despite the careful way they were kept. She wrenched her gaze away as it began to descend to his hips, and encountered the tie he'd already loosened around his neck.

It was almost ten o'clock in the morning and Chance looked as though he'd been working since the crack of dawn. He probably had. He was the hardest worker she'd ever known, always had been. Micah gave herself a mental shake. She couldn't excuse his behavior just because he applied his energy to it.

Chance smiled at her hesitantly. He came forward, his hands outstretched.

"Micah, you're early! Come in, I wasn't expecting you just yet."

He closed the distance quickly, but didn't reach for her.

"I . . . gathered that," she said hesitantly. "I didn't mean to intrude, Chance. But the sec—"

"You, intrude? Never. But I'm sorry you had to catch the lion in his den. It's just"—he shrugged his shoulders indifferently—"business."

She couldn't think of an appropriate response

that didn't sound judgmental. She remained still as they silently measured each other. Last night had been glorious beyond words. Now they were stilted. Too carefully polite.

Chance was the first to speak. "You look lovely, Micah. I like your hair down." He smiled disarmingly and touched the emerald dangling from her lobe. "And you wore the earrings. For me . . . I hope?"

The war waged within. Part of her still abhorring what she'd walked in on; the other half thrilling to the words he spoke so gently, moving her with the lightness of his touch, his notice of such little things.

She started to lie, to say no. But he wouldn't have believed her anyway.

"Yes," she said quietly. "Yes, Chance. I did wear them for you."

He reached for her hands, and this time she didn't draw back. Not even when he bent swiftly to brush his lips over her cheek. The skin prickled on the nape of her neck.

"You just made my day," he said.

She coughed and glanced away, trying to cover up the intimacy that was pulling at her, trying to remind herself why she was here.

"Remember? No special treatment," she teased, trying to ease the building tension. "I just hope the lion doesn't decide to sharpen his claws on me too."

Chance threw his head back and laughed. His laugh was rough, a little alien sounding, and she realized it was a sound she hadn't heard often.

He led her to a sleekly styled chair in front of

his desk, then went around and sat down, forming a steeple with his fingertips.

"So you want to start a business."

"That's right. Something I can call my own."

"It's a jungle out there. Think you can handle it?"

"I don't see that I have much choice. It's either that or starve." She smoothed her hand over her skirt self-consciously and noticed Chance's gaze followed the movement, lingering at her legs. "Besides," she went on, hoping he'd look back up, "I seem to have this driving urge to prove something to myself. I want to accomplish something with my life. It doesn't have to be grand, especially not at first. But I have to start somewhere." As she fidgeted with the hem of her skirt, Chance looked back up and smiled. He was obviously enjoying himself.

"Then I'm glad you came to me. You're right if you think I'm tough. Mean, too, if you ask the right people. But I won't steer you wrong, Micah. And believe it or not, I usually try to be fair. Even where others are concerned."

He reached to the side of his desk and pulled a thick manila folder off a pile of papers that were neatly arranged. Opening the folder, he flipped through several pages before picking up a gold pen that matched half a dozen gold accessories on the heavy mahogany desk. He seemed to be squinting as he went through the papers, then with a scowl, he opened the top drawer and withdrew—glasses?

"Reading glasses," he said, before gliding his finger along the bridge of his nose. He perused the papers while she watched him, feeling for some strange, inexplicable reason that he looked appealingly vulnerable. Especially the way he seemed to disdain them, keeping them hidden as long as possible as though it hurt his pride to be less than perfect.

"I like the glasses, Chance. They make you look—" she tilted her head, considering, "distinguished."

He glanced up from the papers and seemed to be expecting something insincere or teasing in the remark. Finding none, he nodded and grinned.

"Thanks. I hate the damn things. I think they make me look . . . dull as dishwater." He shrugged.

"Dull?" Micah couldn't keep back the hoot of laughter. "You, Chance? Dull? As dishwater? The bad boy of New Orleans is going to hurt his reputation if he keeps talking like that."

He grinned then began to laugh too. "I love to hear you laugh, Micah. If wearing these is what it takes, I'll resign myself to the duration. I'm totally unscrupulous in my methods when it comes to you, you know."

Micah didn't doubt that for one minute, and the laughter died as the truth of that single statement sunk in. Chance seemed to realize his mistake, and covered up the ensuing silence as he poured over the papers once more.

"So," he said. "You're interested in rental property, right?"

One . . . two . . . three . . . the seconds ticked past as Micah absorbed what he'd just said. When had she told Chance about her plans? She couldn't remember . . . because she hadn't. She was sure of it.

"How did *you* know I was interested in rental property?" she asked slowly, not sure she wanted to hear the answer.

He seemed slightly off balance. Just for an instant, before he shrugged nonchalantly.

"Oh," he said easily. "Word gets around in this business. I've got my fingers in a lot of pies. Real estate is the biggest slice. I heard about your deal that fell through. I'm sorry about that, Micah. You know I would have helped if you'd just asked."

Something didn't feel quite right. Even if word did get around, this was a big city. Awfully big for Chance to have known of her business dealings. She had been discreet. She pushed the niggling thought away.

"I appreciate the thought, Chance. But you know how I feel about taking your money."

He held up his hand. "I wasn't offering. Just making a statement." He pulled out the piece of paper he'd been studying and handed it to her. "Take a look at this and tell me what you think."

Micah scanned the page, looking over Chance's distinctive scrawl. Her brow furrowed, and she read it again.

Looking back up, she shook her head. "I told you, Chance. I've only got around three thousand dollars. From reading this I get the distinct impression that not only is the down payment more than I've got, the property needs repair."

"Lots of it. New paint, carpeting. A little plumbing. A lot of carpentry work. And the appliances need replacing, but we could get by with some good used ones."

"Then why are you showing me this? I don't know how to fix a pipe, much less how to hang paneling."

"Not yet, you don't." Chance leaned forward and fixed her with a steady, almost challenging, gaze. "Here are the facts, Micah. You're not going to find *anything* for a few thousand bucks' investment. The best you can do is get something that needs work and haggle for a lower down. This property is basically sound, in an okay neighborhood, but the cosmetics are shot. I've been considering it for the past month or so; so far no one else seems to be interested. The owner wants out. I think it could be a good move for both of us if I cut you in on the deal."

Micah realized she was gripping the paper tightly, and she was fighting the buzzing noise in her head. This seemed like more work than she'd bargained for. But what had she expected? A miracle? That Chance had some kind of magic solution that with a little money, a little work, all her problems would be ended? Grow up, she told herself. Listen to the man, he knows what he's talking about. And she was in no position to argue.

"Go ahead, Chance," she said, feeling uneasier by the minute.

"Here's the plan. You put up what you've got for your portion of the down payment. I'll put up the rest."

"I don't think—"

Chance held up his hand. "Hear me out, Micah, before you say no."

She nodded reluctantly. "All right, I'm listening."

"Good, because I think you'll like the idea once you get used to it. What I want to do is furnish the materials, have some of my men come in for the electrical and plumbing problems. The rest is up to you."

"The rest, meaning . . . ?"

"Hanging the wallpaper. Doing the running, like finding the best buy on carpeting. Painting the interior. Sweat equity, Micah. I furnish the supplies, you furnish part of the labor, and your ideas on color schemes. All that stuff I'd have to pay a decorator for if you didn't do it. When it's done, we resell and find another project, or rent and split the immediate profits."

"But, Chance. I don't know how to hang wallpaper, or . . . or—"

"I do. And I don't mind teaching you how. Something tells me you'd be really good at it."

"But if you're teaching me, I'm not doing my part, and then it's no different from a handout."

His scowl was enough to make her shrink back. But she wouldn't. She didn't care if it was foolish, she had her pride, and she wouldn't allow Chance to supply the charity.

"Get this, Micah. If anyone knows what a handout is, it's me. My mother had to take enough while I was growing up and I'm not about to insult you by offering you one. It's a business deal, pure and simple. In fact, if you'll ditch your pride and come to your senses long enough to see this could be a good move for both of us, I'll have my lawyer draw up the papers. That way you'll *know* it's a legal transaction, not some kind of trumped up excuse for me to give you money you don't want. Believe it or not, I'm still careful with my money. I don't treat *any* investment lightly. Not even one with you."

He swiped his glasses off his nose and tossed them down on the desk. His jaw was set, and Micah could feel her stomach twist as she came toe-to-toe with the infamous shark from the waterfront.

"Now," he continued tersely. "You *said* you wanted to *work* at something you could make a go at. Here's your chance. Take it or leave it."

She carefully laid the paper on his desk in front of her and made the pretense of studying it once more so she could avoid meeting his probing, dark gaze. She could hear him slowly but steadily tapping the pen on the desk, and clasped her hands together, trying to still them from covering the hollow of her throat, just as she forced her feet not to slap the sandal back and forth against her heel.

What was she to do? Did she have a choice? Sure she did. She could turn her back on this opportunity Chance was offering her, just to salvage her pride since he'd been so . . . so business-like. Abrasively so. The way he'd put it to her, she couldn't help but believe he was really looking at it as just that—business. And wasn't that what she'd asked for? No special treatment? She looked up from the paper to see Chance studying her too closely for comfort.

Micah cleared her throat and asked as cooly as possible, "Shall we go look at the property?"

His brooding expression faded as he smiled.

"Thought you'd never ask." He reached for his jacket, turning so she wouldn't see his expression of victory. Or hear the weighty sigh that betrayed his unadulterated relief.

Seven

Micah swiped her fingertip down the molding of the kitchen doorway. Not only was the place dirty, the ghastly purple paint was chipped, revealing a mottled olive-green beneath. It was enough to turn her stomach. And the thin sheen of kitchen grease covering everything did.

She shuddered, and could hear Chance's chuckle close behind her.

"This is what you call a handyman's special. But believe it or not, by the time we finish, this place will sparkle. Buy cheap, rent high. Or sell—but we'll cross that bridge when we come to it."

Micah turned and faced him, unable to keep her distaste, or dubious belief in his claim, to herself.

"But, Chance, it's so . . . so . . ."

"Gross?"

"Yes. Very." She wrinkled her nose, sniffing for anything foul, and was relieved to smell only the sweet scent of honeysuckle and gardenias wafting from the open window above the sink.

"Just look at it this way, Micah. Think of all the satisfaction you'll get when you look at the final product. It makes a person feel good to take a lost cause and turn it around. I'd think that was right up your alley."

He looked at her keenly. Micah looked away, ignoring his not so subtle message.

"You're impossible," she laughed. "And you always manage to get your way with me. How you do it, I don't know, you . . . you scallywag."

Chance clucked his tongue in mock dismay. "Micah, such language. And all heaped on a man who's crazy about you."

The smile faded on her lips, and Chance raised a brow in question.

"Was it something I said?"

"You believe in bringing out the heavy artillery, don't you?"

"Only when the occasion warrants. And believe me, Micah, you ain't seen nothing yet."

He turned away abruptly, directing his attention to the sink. He tried the faucets while she stood there absorbing the last of what she knew she should take as a warning. This was a mistake, getting into a business with Chance. He was going to ensure this "business" alliance was far from just business. Then why wasn't she as upset as she should be? Why was she standing there with such a silly, dreamy look she could even feel on her face?

Get rid of it! She had to do this on her own,

without his help. Tell him. Tell him now before it's too late—

"Chance, we need to talk about this. About—"

"Sure, Micah. But come over here first. I want to show you something."

She'd been ready to say it and get it over with no matter where that left her, only now he was leaning over the faucet, fiddling with the spout.

"Anyone ever show you how to change a washer?"

"A what?"

"A washer. Look. See how this faucet leaks? Here, first I'll turn off the water supply. Okay, here, take this."

Micah reached out and accepted the thin rubber circle Chance held in his palm.

"This is a *washer*?" She examined it curiously. "Hard to imagine how a dinky little piece of rubber like this could stop a leak."

"That's right. Now, watch how I unscrew this piece of the faucet here . . . and you put the washer in there . . . that's good, very good . . . okay, now we screw the cap on the faucet back in place." He handed her the cap. "You do it."

Micah followed his directions, intrigued with the simple job as he talked her through.

She finished and turned the water supply on and Chance turned the faucet.

"Look, Chance! It doesn't leak!"

"Well fancy that. And just think, Micah. You did it *all by yourself*."

"I did, didn't I?" She grinned ear-to-ear with her unexpected accomplishment, then turned to

Chance and impulsively squeezed his hand. "But you helped. You told me what to do."

He squeezed back. "Just investing my time wisely. You can go through later and do the rest by yourself. See how simple this is? I show you how, then you do the rest. Do you still have a problem with that?"

Micah remembered what she'd said about the handout, and could feel herself flush from the misplaced pride.

"No. No, I have no problems with that."

"Good. Now what were you about to say before I called you over here?"

She'd totally forgotten her resolve to call the deal off while they'd worked side by side. But she'd fixed a leaky faucet! It was just a little thing, she knew. But it represented so much. She could learn. So what if Chance had to show her a few tricks of the trade? She'd make it up to him. She'd work so hard there would be no doubt she was doing her part.

No. It was a ridiculous notion to call the deal off when she had this opportunity. And it wasn't charity. As for Chance and what this might mean to their relationship . . . well, that was just the risk she'd have to take.

"Micah?" He broke into her silence.

"Oh, it was nothing. I just wanted to see the rest of the house. Try to get some ideas going on what we need to do to make our money back."

Chance nodded in approval. "Now you're talking. I'll make an offer today and have my lawyers expedite the papers. Right this way . . . *cherie*."

He extended his hand. She hesitated only a

moment before lacing her fingers with his, and tried to ignore the bubble of delight from her accomplishment that lapped into an even greater ripple of pleasure at hearing the name he used to call her so long ago.

"And that, my dear woman, is how you hang wallpaper." Chance laid the wooden roller down and motioned Micah closer. "Your turn."

Micah shook her head as she reached for the pasted sheet of heavy paper. "I don't believe it. Last week it was paneling, this week it's wallpaper. Where in the world did you learn all these things?"

Chance's laugh was a little jagged. "Where in the world is about right. I managed to work my way across Europe doing odd jobs like this." He caught the end that was trying to curl up on itself. "Careful, or you'll have paste on the wrong side. Here, let me get that started for you. I'm taller, which happens to come in handy at the moment."

He took the sheet from her sticky grasp, and Micah couldn't help but notice the way his arm muscles rippled in the sleeveless old football jersey as he strained to reach the upper edge of the wall. The jersey rode up, giving more than a glimpse of the taut dark skin of his waist, the even darker hair tapering from his chest and plunging beneath his jeans. It left her with little doubt that Chance had managed to only get better with age.

"You're not watching . . . at least not where you should be."

Micah's gaze swung upward, encountering an amused, if not possibly smug expression on his face. Her own face colored immediately.

"I . . . I—" She felt foolish, caught like that.

"Yes?"

He raised a brow, throwing her balance off even more as he reached for the roller lying beside her. He leaned down close so that his arm brushed against her bare legs. Despite the shorts she wore, Micah felt next to naked from the contact.

"I was just wondering about Europe."

"What do you want to know?"

Oh, nothing, she wanted to say. Just things like, who were you sleeping with there, what kind of life were you leading while I waited for you to come back?

He stood upright again, brushing her leg once more as he did. He handed Micah the roller and motioned for her to do the honors. She tried to ignore the prickle of gooseflesh, and stepped onto the stool that put them at eye level, then began to roll the air bubbles out.

"When were you there?" So much for the questions she really wanted to ask.

"About two years after I left New Orleans."

"For how long?"

"Long enough." He pried up an edge of the paper and smoothed it out. "Go over that again."

"How long is long enough?"

"You don't give up easy, do you?"

"Not when I want to weasel some information out of you, I don't." She laughed and went over the place he'd indicated. "Besides, you're so mysterious about it, you made me curious."

"Did it ever occur to you maybe there's a reason for that?"

"What, did you end up on the wrong side of a gun when a peasant farmer caught you with his daughter?"

She meant for her words to come out lightly, a joke. But instead the words hung suspended and heavy. She looked straight ahead at the wall.

Chance caught the hand she had clutched tight about the roller. Her movements had stilled, and slowly, steadily he began the up-and-down motions again. His chest was so close to her back, she could hear his breathing, feel the heat of their bodies mingling, though nothing touched but his hand at her wrist.

"Is that what you think?" he said quietly, close to her ear.

She shivered at the wisp of his breath fanning her neck. Her eyes shut, letting him lead her strokes, reveling in their closeness, the deep rumble of his voice.

"There were others, I'm sure."

"Naturally," he said.

Don't think about it. Don't wonder if they were blond or dark or what secrets he'd shared with them.

"So . . Europe must have been a cornucopia of pleasures."

"Not exactly." He chuckled. "More like a three-year stint in the fine art of working my butt off. In France I tended grapes. Rome found me waiting tables. When I got tired of that, I laid bricks for a living in Germany. And when I got to Switzerland, well . . ."

"Switzerland?" she prompted.

"Switzerland," he sighed, "'is where I landed a job transporting cargo for a wealthy investor. He was going to teach me the ropes, how to get a business going, that kind of stuff. Hell, I thought I'd landed in a gold mine—found the ticket to success that had escaped me everywhere else I'd looked."

Chance stopped working the roller, but he still kept hold of her wrist. Stroking the pulse beating faster now.

"He taught me some things all right. Such as how to launder dirty money coming in from the States, how to set up scams and cover yourself so the authorities couldn't track you down. Wonderfully ethical business ventures like that."

Micah swallowed hard. Chance's nearness was doing a number on her senses, even as his revelation was managing to unsettle her stomach.

"Were you a quick study?" she asked hesitantly.

"Oh, yeah. Real quick. I caught on fast enough to know that I was being set up to take a fall for the boss. Seems someone had caught whiff of stolen paintings being transported over the border. Funny how he trusted me, his newest employee, more than anyone else to take the next shipment. He assumed, of course, I hadn't figured out the truth."

Micah turned quickly, nearly upsetting her balance, and Chance caught her to him. Their faces were close, and their breasts pressed evenly against each other. Hearts beat quickly, heavily in countertime.

"What happened?"

"I took a powder."

"You mean you left?"

"Caught a flight to the Middle East and dropped out of sight. But not before I took an advance on the job and put an anonymous call through to the authorities on the case. The man was a jerk, and an unethical jerk at that. Made me look like a choirboy. In fact, he probably had a lot to do with reforming that streak of hellion in me. By the time I was drilling oil with the Saudis, I'd had my fill of illegal ventures. Knowing how close I'd come to spending time behind bars managed to knock some sense into me. Not only that, but I learned it gave me a sick feeling to steal from other people—no matter how white the paper was that handled the nasty transaction."

Micah laid her free hand over his shoulder, feeling the solidness of him. People had said so many evil things about Chance through the years that his story wasn't what she'd expected.

"And what about the Saudis? What was your life like there?" Although she'd learned a lot about him over the past minutes, she didn't really find out what she wanted to know. He had revealed nothing about his personal life.

"The Saudis, young lady, are yet another chapter in the *Mysterious Adventures of Chance Renault.*" He smiled suddenly and tweaked her nose. "Save your breath, Micah. You're only allotted one chapter per interrogation."

She took a deep breath. "But I still have a question about Switzerland."

Chance's smile faded. He ran his knuckles against the ridge of her jaw.

"No, Micah. There wasn't anyone special there, if that's what you're asking." His gaze flicked over her, lingering on her hair. He tucked a curl behind her ear. "Besides, there weren't many around with dark hair and green eyes."

A flush of pleasure swept through her at the implied compliment, but Chance suddenly moved away. Picking up the next sheet of wallpaper, he handed it to her.

"Let's get crackin'. At this rate we'll be hanging paper next month. And my stomach's already growling for that dinner you promised me tomorrow night."

"But, Chance, what did you—"

"I'll make some more paste in the kitchen. Try not to let it overlap while I'm gone."

"But, Chance—"

"Be careful to match the pattern. And don't forget to enjoy this—"

"But—"

"Because next week you learn to cut tile."

Micah opened the door leading out back, cursing profusely at the fumes invading the kitchen. Cooking was never her specialty and in her excitement she had managed to do even worse than usual—namely, forgetting to take the stuffed Cornish hens out of the oven. Even now billows of smoke rose to the high ceiling while the charred hens lay in state beside the sink.

"Damn, damn, *damn!*" So much for impressing Chance. And worst of all she'd broken down and decided to turn on the air conditioner only to have the air go out the back—

"What the hell . . where's the fire?"

Micah whirled around, the wet towel she was flapping furiously, clutched in her hands.

"What are you doing here? You're not due for"—she took a glance at the kitchen clock—"five minutes." She motioned toward the back door he'd come through. "And you're supposed to use the front door. Now go sit out there while I tend to this. There is no fire, just a little smoke."

"A *little* smoke? You could pass out from the fumes in here." Chance strode over to the offending oven and closed its door, muttering something about grease and broilers not mixing. "And another thing," he threw over his shoulder, "if you want me to use the front door, you've got to answer it." He whirled back around and faced her.

For a minute they shared a belligerent stare. Micah wasn't sure who cracked the first smile, but soon they were both chuckling. She pointed to the back door.

"Now, would you please pretend you were never here and go back the way you came? You're due in one minute and I don't want to miss answering the door."

"Yes, ma'am." He gave a smart salute before exiting with his coat. Just as she slumped against the kitchen sink, he poked his head around the door frame. "And by the way, blackened redfish is one of my favorite dishes. Never thought I'd get a chance to try out blackened hens. You must be a real whiz in the kitchen, Micah, thinking up things Paul Prudhomme and Julia Child put together couldn't come up with."

He ducked quickly as the wet towel slapped beside the frame. Micah could still hear his laughter as he rounded the outside corner of the house. She wished she could be mad at him—he really was a beast.

She glanced morosely at the hens, sighed, and headed through the swinging doors. She had a terrible suspicion that she smelled vaguely of smoke.

Micah stood in the entryway, just as Chance rapped twice on the front door. The leaded glass on either side distorted his figure, and she imagined him standing there years before, a wildcat with a leather jacket. Taking a deep breath, she twisted the heavy gold knob.

" 'Evening, Micah."

"Good evening, Chance."

He propped his arm on the entry frame, stopping short of entering. No leather jacket this time, he was darkly handsome in his finely tailored clothes.

"You look good to me."

"Thank you. You're not so bad yourself."

"May I come in?"

"Please, do."

She moved aside and he stepped over the threshold, stopping for a moment, as though savoring a victory. She followed his gaze as he looked up toward the banister, where she'd stood that night. When his gaze met hers again, it was hooded, serious.

"I could get used to this," he said.

"Could you?" She could, too, she realized. And all too easily, at that.

Suddenly he looked perplexed and he cocked his head, sniffing.

"Mmmm. Smells like someone's been cooking. Can't wait to see what's for dinner."

"It's a new recipe. Blackened Cornish game hens. I hope you like it."

Micah didn't bother to hide her mischievous smile or the glitter of amusement in her eyes. He'd be crying for McDonald's long before she was through.

Chance laughed and extended his arm.

"Why don't you show me to the parlor? I prefer to eat my crow in there."

Eight

Chance studied Micah as she poured the coffee out of the silver service. He thought the demitasse set ridiculous, but had to admire the practiced grace of her movements. Micah looked every inch the proud Southern lady as she sat beside him on the Victorian couch daintily sipping at the hot liquid; he, however, felt like Goliath cradling a midget's teacup in his palm. Two gulps and he set it down.

"More?" she inquired.

"No thanks. That topped the dinner off just fine."

"Why, you . . . you rat!" She chuckled and set hers down, then took a playful punch at his arm. "You're a worse tease now than when we were kids, Chance Renault."

"Like the song says, 'I was so much older then,' and believe me I am younger than that now." Chance stretched his arms out over his head, then nonchalantly draped one around the back of her neck. He smiled as she shifted closer to him while pretending she wasn't. It reminded him of the old days, back when nice girls gave the "okay" signal without taking the initiative.

Apparently Micah needed a reminder about their little bargain. After all, he had promised to let her call the shots. Then again, he wasn't exactly above manipulating her into asking for it either.

His finger teased at the nape of her neck, toying with the fine hairs there. She shivered. He moved his hand away, resting it on the back of the couch. She looked up at him, questioningly.

"Something wrong, *ma cherie*?"

She hesitated. "No . . . I just . . . well, I liked what you were doing."

Her cheeks turned pink, as he knew they would. Her voice was higher, softer than usual too. His body responded to the vulnerability in her.

"Oh? Then you don't want me to stop?" His fingers found their way back, continuing their playful taunt.

The silence lengthened. He was content . . . almost. A sigh escaped from Micah, and he began to slowly rub her tendons that were tensed beneath his palm.

"Nice?" he asked quietly. She nodded. "If you like the way it feels, you have to say so . . . it's part of the rules."

"Yes," she said. The word came out in one languorous, sensual syllable. And then as if she had given away too much, the muscles he had coaxed to relax flexed tight again.

"Do you remember the first time we met?" she said suddenly, turning just enough to peer up at him.

Chance squelched the urge to scowl at her. Patience, he told himself, patience. The heightened color of her skin, the evasive but hazy cast to her eyes, and most of all the sight of her nipples jutting beneath the silk of her blouse . . . combined to give him the momentary patience he needed.

Chance raised his eyes from her chest to her face again. Her breathing quickened, and he smiled slowly, satisfied that he could so easily rattle her.

"Remember?" he finally said. "How could I ever forget? You were the cutest kid in pigtails I'd ever seen, sobbing your heart out in the backyard because your kitten was stuck in the tree. It just happened to be the one tree your parents forbade you to climb."

"You weren't supposed to climb it either," she pointed out.

"Which only made it that much more tempting."

He leaned his head back against the faded brocade fabric and stared up at the lofty crystal chandelier. It felt strange being in this room. Time seemed to stand still here. He could remember peeking from the kitchen where his mother was working, and her scolding him to get back where he belonged. Some things still hurt to think about.

"I'll never forget your mother running out there, fussing at you for ripping your jeans. I thought you were a hero, the way you saved my kitten . . .

the way you took the blame on yourself instead of putting it off on me. That image stuck for a long time."

He looked away from the ceiling, putting the unhappy memories behind him. Better to think of Micah, she was here now. "Yeah, I guess it did, for both of us. It did wonders for my ego when everyone else said I wouldn't amount to anything but trouble, and you thought I'd hung the moon."

"That's exactly what I thought," she said. "I felt special that someone older than me would take the time to play with me. Of course, as you grew up there were times you had to act tough and not pay much attention to me in front of your friends. Once, I went home and cried. I wrote a page about it in my diary."

Chance shook his head. He relished the feel of her beneath his fingertips, the way she began to lean into the massage he was giving her shoulders. He tried to concentrate on that instead of the feelings of futility and confusion the memory could evoke even now.

"That wasn't an easy choice for me. Even when you were barely in your teens I knew I had it bad. But you weren't only off-limits because of your family, you were too young."

Micah lowered her lashes. "But I didn't stay off-limits." She looked back up.

He nodded slowly. His mouth settled in a half-smile.

"My conscience told me what I was doing was wrong—but somehow I was never able to make myself feel remorse for one of the most wonderful experiences of my life."

Chance leaned over and switched off the antique lamp to Micah's left. Only the entry light gave a faint glow to the darkness.

But the dark couldn't mask the rapid rasp of her breath—or maybe it was the dark magnifying the silence around their breathing.

"I want to lie down beside you," he whispered. "And I want to hold you . . . that's all." Like hell, that's all, screamed every instinct he possessed as she bent back, resting against the feathered cushions. She hadn't hesitated at all. She trusted him, he realized. It was the same trust she had given him so long ago. The movement was too familiar, a nostalgia that was too acute, too painfully sweet.

Chance felt the swell of emotion in his throat; the even thicker swell of his groin. He moved until her head rested on his chest, his arm secure about her shoulders. She sighed in contentment, and he tried not to groan as she shifted and brushed against his hardness. Micah stiffened at the contact, and for a horrible, frozen moment he thought she might jerk free of his hold. He had a good idea she was fighting her own similar responses.

"Chance, I'm sorry. Maybe we shouldn't—"

"Shhh. It's okay . . . it's okay." He brought her head back to his chest, fighting the urge to roll her beneath him, to seduce her right there. Instead, he began to stroke through her hair, forcing his voice to soothe, yet unable to hide the hoarseness of desire.

"Sometimes it's hard for me to believe we've

The Editors of Loveswept Romances invite you to:

CLAIM A FREE SURPRISE GIFT...

Lift Here

...PLUS SIX FREE ROMANCES!

6 ROMANCES FREE

Detach and affix this stamp to the postage-paid reply card — and mail at once!

NO OBLIGATION TO BUY!

THE FREE GIFTS ARE YOURS TO KEEP

SEE DETAILS INSIDE ➡

YOU GET SIX ROMANCES FREE...
Plus A SURPRISE GIFT!

Loveswept Romances

AFFIX
FREE
BOOKS
STAMP
HERE.

A beautiful golden rope necklace and bracelet set!

This FREE gift is yours to keep.

MY "NO RISK" GUARANTEE

There's no obligation to buy — the free gifts are mine to keep. I may preview each subsequent shipment for 15 days. If I don't want it, I simply return the books within 15 days and owe nothing. If I keep them, I will pay just $2.09 per book. (I save $2.50 off the retail price for the 6 books) plus postage and handling, and sales tax where applicable.

YES! Please send my six Loveswept novels FREE along with my FREE GIFT described inside the heart!

Item #40709

NAME_____

ADDRESS_____APT_____

CITY_____

STATE_____ZIP_____

BR789

enough now that he could feel the wisp of her breath as she spoke. Sweet, warm breath that still managed to take his away.

"Tell me about it . . . about Saudi."

"Saudi was . . . quite an adventure."

He was glad it was dark. She wouldn't be able to see the tautening of his features as he spoke. Hopefully she wouldn't sense it either.

"Was it glamorous there? Exciting? Did you see sheikhs and camels?"

"Oh yeah, it was glamorous all right. Like something most people only dream about. A page right out of *The Arabian Nights*."

Did she believe that? A dream? It had been a nightmare. Hot. Dirty. Sweating as if he were a faucet, doing fourteen-hour days. "Just paradise, Micah," he said.

The shortness of his tone echoed between them. Neither said anything for a few strained moments.

"You're lying. Tell me the truth, Chance."

Could he? No one knew about those lonely, dark years. Especially not Micah.

"You really get to me, lady, you know that?"

She hesitated, then, "You get to me, too, Chance."

What those words did to him. Warm, sweet. Good. Like her. Lord, what he wouldn't give to bury himself inside her, to take the healing warmth her body offered . . .

He rolled her beneath him. Micah's breath caught.

He pressed himself hard against the vee of her thighs, lying there still, atop her, making her feel him, the length and breadth of his need. No, he couldn't begin the movements. If he did, there would be no stopping. For this one thing, *she* must ask. His reasons were selfish—but then again, *he* was selfish.

"Ask me to kiss you," he whispered urgently, and cupped her face in his hands with a gentle pressure.

She ignored his plea. "What was it like there?" she said, then rushed on as though compelled to know some horrible secret he kept. "How many women did you ask to kiss you there? You left me alone too many nights, too damn many years wondering just that, Chance. How many miserable hours did I spend wondering where you were, who you were with, while I was waiting—" her voice broke, he could feel the warm trek of tears streaming between his palms. "Waiting for you to come back to me."

He felt the tears run down her face, rubbing the moisture against his skin, loving it. Rejoicing that she could still feel so deeply about him.

"Where was I?" he murmured. "Chasing a dream. It was you, Micah. You were the dream that kept me going when I wanted to quit. And yes, there were other women. Ones with long black hair and cat-green eyes. Ones that didn't mind me calling them by someone else's name—"

She gasped, and he took a perverse pleasure in showing her the uglier side of his world; let her see him as he really was. Let her love him despite it. Nothing less would do.

"Only that changed when I came back," he said. "When I was finally able to offer you some kind of life. But you were married and I didn't care who I slept with. I used other women to punish you for being unfaithful to me. But I always pretended the others were you." Now he did move into her. His body stretched possessively, hungrily over hers.

"I needed you." Her voice shook. She shook. In fury? In passion? He didn't know. "And you never came back. Not until it was too late. Why, Chance? *Why*?"

"Why? Because I knew if I had even a taste, I wouldn't be able to tear myself away, to go back and do what I had to."

"I would have gone away with you. In a minute, Chance. You shouldn't have made my decision for me. It wasn't your right. Not after I was old enough to leave."

"No? What was I going to do? Bring you along for a joyride on the rigs? Or maybe just swathe you in soiled linens at the flophouses. That would have really impressed you. I might not have had two cents to my name, but I had pride, Micah. I would have stayed away for good before letting you see me like that. Or worse, offered you that kind of life. That decision was my right. I had the right to leave you where you belonged—in college, with your family. Leading a normal existence. Not shacking up with a loser."

"You were *never* a loser, Chance," she said fiercely. "A card, a call, any kind of sign, and I would have come to you. None of it would have mattered, not as long as we were together."

The tears had stopped. Her voice was quiet, but

firm. He needed this—this equality of her subtle strength answering the hardness of his.

"That's right. You would have come to me. And it *would* have mattered. Feel this?" He thrust into her, the clothes doing nothing to mute the degree of his arousal. Her breath caught, but she said nothing. "I said, Micah, 'do you feel . . . this?' "

"Yes," she whispered sharply.

"And you like the way it feels, don't you?"

"*Yes,*" she hissed.

He tried not to gloat when she instinctively rose to meet the next thrust. He took a deep breath and stopped. With all his will he forced himself to stop, not to rip their clothes away.

"Well, let me tell you something. It feels mighty good on this comfortable couch, in this nice cool room. But I can guarantee you, it would only have been a matter of time before you started to hate it . . . To hate me. To dread the feel of my body on yours in a flea-bitten shack, while I got more bitter by the day for not achieving the kind of life I craved. You can't climb the ladder from the bottom up when it's hand-to-mouth, and you have more than one mouth to feed."

"It wouldn't have been like that. How can you even say such things, Chance?"

"How?" he snorted. "Don't you kid yourself. You can't see it, because you didn't grow up in poverty. On the other side of the tracks kids turn tricks, dropouts do drugs, and most of us never know who our old man was. And the ones who do stick around blow the welfare check on pure grain then beat up their wives. That's the reality of it, Micah. That was the neighborhood I grew up in."

The room was suddenly so still, like the aftermath of destruction. He waited, glad he'd spelled it out, yet wishing he hadn't. Maybe it was more than she could accept, maybe she could only care for the shiny new penny, the bright, successful man he had become. He'd always wanted it all, prayed that she could take all of him, and not just what everyone else saw. Maybe, just maybe, he wanted too much.

The softness of her body beneath him, the sweet rasp of her breath against his face obliterated the shadow of ugliness past. It was the memory of her that had brought him this far. This was *his* Micah. His only love.

He gathered her close. He'd take what he could get.

"I'm sorry, Micah. I never meant to tell you all this. You were never meant to—"

"Never meant to what—see your life? Live the way you did? You were wrong, Chance. I never would have hated you." She wrapped her arms around his neck, and he could feel his spirit soar, his heart swell with an emotion that was savagely possessive. "I never would have dreaded you touching me. And you never would have been bitter. I wouldn't have let you. We would have worked together. We would have sacrificed together. Somehow everything would have worked out, and neither of us would be lying here now with the regrets the years have been so generous with. You've made your mistakes, and I've made mine. Well, I'm tired of mistakes. I'm not about to make one now."

"No? And just what mistake would that be?"

He held his breath in anticipation. His hands—hands that hadn't quavered in the face of violence—vaguely shook.

Micah pulled his head down to her own. "Not asking you to kiss me," she whispered against his mouth.

The lips that met his were hungry, tender, and bold. The skimming of mouths, the mating of tongues. And the whimpering sounds she couldn't mute, the answering growls he made no effort to restrain.

His lips skimmed the length of her neck, tonguing the pulse that beat wildly in the warm hollow. She held him close, and urged him on, pressing him closer. His hands reached for the buttons of her blouse, and he forced himself to move slowly, though he wanted to tear them away. Her hands treaded through his hair greedily; he welcomed the tug, the slight discomfort.

If only there were a candle, even some small light to let him see the miracle of what he was feeling. Her breasts, so full and heavy as he fondled them through the gossamer silk of her bra, needed to be suckled—this she told him with no more than the upward tilt of buds he remembered to be the color of roses.

"Remember the first time I kissed you there?" he whispered against the wet silk, raising the flesh beneath his mouth.

"I remember," she whispered shakily.

"And do you remember the first time I undressed you?"

"The only time . . . yes. I could never forget."

The blouse was gone now, so too the bra. He rubbed his chest against her, feeling the fabric of his shirt graze the soft nudity of her flesh; he relished the way her breasts rolled beneath the expanse of him. He lowered his head once more and laved them, then unable to help himself, he moved so that his hand skimmed beneath her skirt. Her legs were parted, and insistently he tried to nudge them wider.

She clamped her legs tight, capturing his hand between them as though she were still a virgin protecting the barrier. He laughed quietly, seductively.

"You did the same thing when I had you against the car before we went parking. But you opened them for me before the night was through." He massaged the bone beneath his palm, feeling the silk of panties covering her, silk that was unable to hide the evidence of moisture against his trapped fingers. He moved them to excite her, to caress her, and persuade, using the fabric to tease the velvet texture he ached to more intimately touch.

"Chance," she whispered. "Chance, it's too soon. Once this starts, we'll never be able to quit."

"You're right. And you don't really want me to stop now, do you? We know how good it is with us, how it's always been . . . always will be. Tell me not to stop. Tell me you're ready to pick up the pieces, to make love the way we should have all those years instead of wasting it on other people."

He heard the quickening of her breath, the sign of heightened arousal sliding wetly against his fingertips. He needed her—Lord, how he needed her—and he would do whatever it took to take what he needed. Deftly he rolled a nipple over his tongue and between his teeth. Before she could refuse, he breached the barrier of the panties, sliding his fingers around the elastic. Into the heat he slipped them, deep inside. The pounding of blood rushed through his veins at the contact; the hated prison of his pants cloaked the pulse of his virility, which moved in an insistent rhythm against her thigh.

"There's no one else now, Micah . . . there's just us. Ask me to undress you, that's all you have to do. Just two simple words, 'undress me,' and we'll share something wonderful again . . . something sacred." He flexed his fingers. She gasped; contracted. He did it again.

"Chance . . . please. . . ."

He smiled in the dark. So ready to take her, to make her his own.

"Please . . . not yet . . . I . . . I need more time."

The dark swallowed his curse. He withdrew his hand and sat up. Abruptly, before she could cover her breasts, or push down the bunched fabric of her skirt, he leaned over and turned on the lamp, not caring if she minded. His eyes feasted while they could, challenging the startled irises of green to deny him this.

"You're beautiful." He growled the words like an accusation. "Not tonight . . . but one day I won't have to ask. One day, Micah, you'll be mine. Each rosy-tipped breast, each shuddering contraction . . . mine."

She sat up, pushing her skirt primly over the knees, and crossed her arms over her chest, while moving for the blouse, the bra. He brushed her hands away as they reached, and picked the garments up for her.

"I can dress myself." Her voice wavered in spite of the assertion.

"I'm sure you can. But tonight, let me. If I can't take you to bed, at least let me do something I've imagined a thousand times or more."

Gently, in amazing contrast to the harshness of his voice, he replaced the clothes, inhaling the scent of her body that clung to them. Doing it slowly, making it last.

His only consolation on the lonely ride home, and in the stark solitude of his bed, was the fine tremble he remembered as she let him dress her; and the silent tear that escaped as he kissed her forehead tenderly and whispered, "Good-night."

Nine

"Roll, you jerk! I said, *roll*, damn you!" Micah gave the long-handled stick another shove over the ceiling. The round brush skidded obstinately and plopped yet another big dollop of white over the paint-spattered T-shirt she wore. It did the same to the kerchief covering her head.

She made a noise that was somewhere between a curse, a groan, and a sob.

"Oh, excuse me. I must have taken a wrong turn. Here I came looking for a lady of high society, and ended up with a sailor on the wrong side of the deck. The foul language always gives them away."

Micah swung around at the sound of his voice. She was used to his impromptu visits, but it was a constant source of irritation that he always managed to come when she was in the middle of an impossible mess—most of them worse than the botched dinner and what had followed.

Micah shivered in spite of the hot room. Chance

had dressed her so tenderly, she had wanted to beg him to stop, to undo the buttons once more. And when he had driven away, it was torment the way he had left her hungering for him: Body and mind and spirit. It was getting harder and harder to remember just what it was she was trying to prove; and that fact alone irked her. Suddenly she felt a prickle of anger. It must be the heat. Yes, the heat of the house, not the heat he was inciting by simply standing there.

"Couldn't you call or at least knock first?" she muttered crossly.

"It's my house too." He dangled his copy of the house key.

They stared at each other in what seemed a standoff for a few moments before Chance began to chuckle.

"You've got paint on your head."

"I know."

"And on your arms."

"So what's new?"

"Not to mention, your clothes look like they've been whitewashed."

"Enough, Chance. If I decide I want your opinion on my appearance, I'll ask for it."

"I'll give it to you anyway. Anyone told you lately you look good enough to eat?"

"Stop it, Chance!"

"I'm glad I'm the only one then. I'd hate to get messy by beating someone up for trespassing on my turf."

"Chance. . . ." So she was his turf, was she? The man was impossible! Maddening! To even have the gall to say he didn't want to get *messy* while she stood there with paint from her head to her toes and he just sauntered around in his fresh linen business suit.

Micah pointed the uncooperative paintbrush at him. "Messy?" she repeated. "I'll give you messy, by golly. You come one step closer and we'll look like the Bobbsey Twins. Now go away and don't come back until you're dressed for the occasion."

She slapped the roller back into the once-silver container that was now thickly coated in white. After it was loaded, she deliberately ignored him, and pushed the roller against the ceiling once again, silently praying just this once it would go on right as he watched. She'd show him! She was good at this. The next time she might run away screaming if she had to buy yet another supply of white paint, rollers, and masking tape—but, by gosh, this time she'd show him, that was all.

"You know, it would help if you loosened the screw beside the roller. Then it might actually roll instead of—"

She whirled around and fixed him with a lethal stare.

"Yes?" she said testily. Down came the roller, the stick thudding squarely against the drop cloth. Micah held it like a staff meant to do bodily harm to anyone who got in her way.

Chance shrugged, and she thought she saw the hint of a smile tug at his lips. If he dared to smile at her predicament now, she just might be obliged to share the wealth. Fancy suit or no.

Looking at him standing there so immaculately dressed—his hair neatly brushed, and more than likely remnants of air-conditioning still clinging to his skin while the big box fan was coursing a humid breeze around the room—gave her an almost overwhelming urge to wipe that big, stupid grin off his face. A grin, yes. The man was most definitely grinning.

"You're grinning," she accused.

"Is that a crime?"

"Around here it is. Please take that silly smirk along with your Gucci shoes out of my sight. Or else."

He quirked an eyebrow, and his grin grew wider. "Or else . . . what?"

"Or else I'll belt you with *this*." She hoisted the sodden roller.

"My goodness, Micah, you're touchy today. Sorry the air-conditioning's down . . . it must be the heat."

"I'll give you heat." She jabbed the roller in his vicinity.

"Promises, promises." He started in her direction. "Come on, Micah. Show me a little heat."

"I'm warning you. Get back unless you—"

"Unless I what? Want to find out just how *hot* you can get?"

"Why don't you just keep your nasty thoughts to yourself, you . . . *you*—" She took a threatening step forward.

"Scallywag?" Chance stopped a few inches away from her dubious weapon and touched his finger to the sopping roller.

"Yes! And—"

"Riffraff?" In the blink of an eye he grabbed hold of the stick attached to the roller and jerked it out of her grasp, sending it sailing across the room. Micah watched in horror as it hit against her newly painted wall. The roller left a blob of white over the peach tint she'd put on the day before.

"My wall!" she gasped. "Just look at what you did to my wall!"

"Oops."

"*Oops?* I spent *hours* on these walls yesterday, and all you can say is *oops?*" Impulsively she lunged at him, throwing her paint-streaked body heedlessly against his expensive suit.

"How dare you!" she raged, striking a white hand against his chest. "There you sit, day after day, week after week, shuffling papers behind your cozy little desk, probably drinking café au lait out of your silver chalice. While I'm sweltering here, painting, grouting, tiling, papering . . . you name it! Do you have any idea when the last time was I dressed in something more elegant than a T-shirt and beat-up jeans? No, of course not, because you're too busy in your air-conditioned office, wearing your ritzy Italian silk ties, your pompous Georgio Armani suits—"

Micah's eyes suddenly riveted to where her fists clenched his jacket, the white imprint of a hand on his tailored shirt.

"Your suit! Chance, I've ruined your suit! Oh, no . . . quick! Let's get to the bathroom, maybe if we hurry I can get it—"

"Micah." Chance stilled her frantic attempts to pull away, drawing her closer instead. One hand smoothed down her spine before catching her around the waist. "I don't care about my suit. I care about you." His other hand came up to tilt her face to his.

Unshed tears sparkled in her eyes. Ridiculous. How could she further disgrace herself by crying at a time like this?

"What's wrong, *ma cherie*? Tell me what's troubling you."

And then she did disgrace herself. The tears, hot and stinging, burned the back of her throat as she tried to close them off. But in spite of her most valiant efforts they broke loose.

Chance made a shushing sound and rocked her back and forth against him in what was meant as a comforting gesture. Her head against his chest, he rubbed her back soothingly.

"There now," he murmured, "There now." And it was such a small thing, this paternal inflection she had never seen in him before, that made her suddenly think of what he would be like as a father. Loving, fair . . . but sometimes unbending. A good father, to make up for the one he hadn't had.

The old feelings flooded through her, the ones she couldn't control or ignore. But there was more, something in him she hadn't considered before this moment. And it made him all the more desirable. She was tired of the tug-of-war between her head and her heart that went on every time they were in the same room. Even when they weren't.

No more words were spoken, but she raised her face to his, and reached for him.

"Chance," she whispered. "Please . . . I need—"

That was all it took, as though he had been

waiting on edge for these very words since the night on her couch over three weeks before.

She opened her mouth, invitingly, drawing him deeper.

He wanted her to give. Even as she took, she knew he did, the way he urged her tongue to trail the path of his own. The haze beat wildly, mercilessly through the flame coursing her veins. Damn the defenses, the plague of too much thought. She let him take her to a place they had been before, where instinct and desire ruled; a place where innocence was lost, where she embraced the joy, the exquisite fury of untender love.

"Touch me," she moaned against his mouth, not caring if she pleaded. *Take me. Burn me. Make me your own.* He had to put his hands on her, to mold her curves to his sleek, hard thighs. She had waited for too long, this slow burning to cinders and ash, this hollow want that cradled her when all she really wanted was him.

In the agony of the small moment when his hand was moving, she caught it, brought it to her lips, and kissed it. His hands, his beautiful, work-worn hands were hers for now. She loved them, just as she loved him.

And she did love him. She didn't care anymore who he was to anyone else, only that now he was hers completely. In all his goodness, his badness, his wonderful complexity, she did love him. She'd never stopped. No, never . . .

"Oh, Micah," he groaned, his eyes slitting open. "Micah, I—"

He stilled abruptly, the fallen kerchief lying like an accusing, dead weight on the floor.

His brows drew together, and his mouth, swollen from their kisses, slanted disapprovingly.

"You cut your hair." She heard the regret in his voice. The sound seemed misplaced in the sudden, wilting stillness that continued to crackle with the hum of sexual tension.

Micah touched the short-cropped curls, suddenly self-conscious. She hated the cut, too, had hated it as soon as it was done. That had been the reason she had lashed out at him earlier, trying to transfer the disappointment.

Too late, she wished for her long hair back.

She sniffled; she was being ridiculous. But Chance was looking at her with such visible disappointment, while his hand, the one that even now should be caressing her breast, hovered beside her head.

"I was so hot. Here, at home . . ." she lifted her chin. "Please don't look at me like that. I hate the way it looks, and you're making it worse." She was still aching with longing, and at the same time stinging with the knowledge that he didn't like what he saw. His reaction was the most deflating blow of all. Worse than the heat, or the frustration of her work. She wanted Chance to pretend he liked her hair whether he did or not. And most of all she wanted to grab the moment back, so that he held her until she didn't care about paint or the heat or especially not the cut of her hair.

"I'm vain." She looked away. "I wish I looked better for you. You only see me like this these days, like a drudge. And now . . . you don't even want to touch my hair."

Her voice caught. She hated feeling like this, robbed of some feminine extension. Silly. Vain. Where was her pride, letting him see her so emotionally naked over something so trivial?

Chance caught her shoulders and pulled her to him as she pushed away. Then slowly, very deliberately, he brought his hand to her hair. She tried to pull back in some idiotic surge of pride when his touching her was what she really wanted.

One of his arms slid around to her back until he braced his hand at the nape of her neck, immobilizing her head. His eyes searched hers as though he were looking for something he'd lost, and then skimmed to the short, dark locks as his fingers lightly touched their springy texture. And then he was stroking his fingertips through, watching the waves of onyx tread between them.

The sensation sent a trickle of chills from the roots of her hair to the soles of her feet, and culminated in between.

"I love your hair," he murmured huskily.

She swallowed hard, thrilling to the words. It didn't matter whether they were true or not. "No you don't," she said. "You're just saying that to make me feel better. But . . . it's nice to hear you say it just the same."

There was a rumbling sound that came from his throat—not a chuckle, not even a satisfied murmur.

"I do love it. Because you care enough that it matters what I think."

He pressed his lips against the soft curls, and

then again next to her temple. She still wanted to cry. But this time from joy.

He pulled away and looked at her then, holding her out just far enough to look her up and down.

"Let's put this stuff up. I'll help."

There was such a tender expression on his face.

"But I'm not through yet."

"Yes you are. We're taking the rest of the day off. From the looks of you, it's going to take at least an hour to get cleaned up and put your best clothes on. Enough of this scullery maid duty. You're the classiest number this side of the river. And tonight you're switching colors."

"I'm what?" Baffled, but laughing anyway, she followed his lead and went to pick up the fallen paint roller.

"Colors, I said." He swatted her unceremoniously on her white paint-stained rear end. Micah whirled around with a gasp just before he hoisted her over his shoulder and picked up the roller all in one swoop.

"Tonight, *ma cher*, we're painting the town *red*."

Ten

The opulence of the Louis XIV French restaurant blended marvelously with the evening's mood of romance. Romance, and some feeling of joy that was almost frightening in its anticipation.

She was wearing her best perfume—the last precious few drops she'd saved for . . . *this* night. Micah let herself admit it. Deep down in her heart of hearts she'd known it would come to this. And when she'd reached for the bottle, she knew exactly how it would make her feel: Elegant, womanly, pampered . . . feelings she'd lost for a long time.

It was the secret knowledge that she wanted to wear it for Chance, to stir him with the hint of sensual sweetness pressed behind her ears, in the hollow of her neck, her wrists. And other more intimate places.

Beneath the elegantly set table, she extended one shapely, long leg, and innocently, deliberately, brushed the silk of her hose against the smooth fabric of his trousers. Chance's eyes were dark, probing, but held no mysteries.

Across the linen cloth of the table, he reached for her hand. Micah's fingers curled into his strong ones. She hooked their tapered length, the deep polish of her nails covering the bits of paint she hadn't been able to completely wash away. She could feel the surge of anticipation mounting, trying to revel only in that, and push away the thoughts she knew would have to be spoken before they could consummate this night.

The sound of a throat being cleared brought them out of their mutual, silent trance.

"Wine, monsieur?"

"A bottle of Perrier-Jouët. The '82 vintage, please. And make it well chilled."

"Of course, monsieur."

The waiter left, and Micah couldn't help but smile.

"Sounds like you know your wine."

"A bit. But I've been practicing."

"Oh? I'm impressed."

"Good. I meant for you to be." He laughed at his own self-depreciation. "In fact, I've been practicing things for years with that in mind. Just waiting for the opportunity to show off my acquired panache. I wasn't exactly the smoothest operator around when we were kids."

"I thought you were smooth. And very worldly."

"And I thought you were spun sugar wrapped in a package of dynamite. Sweet, but sexy enough to keep my teenage hormones running in overdrive. Only you were always just out of my reach."

She shook her head. "You just thought I was."

"No. Back then you really were. But not anymore."

The waiter appeared and presented the bottle of champagne, serving it with proper finesse. She actually preferred Mimosas, but there would be something profane about mixing orange juice into this vintage.

Chance tested it with skill and ease, then nodded for Micah to receive the first glass. The ritual done, he turned to her as the waiter settled the bottle into the champagne bucket of crushed ice.

"Now watch closely while I order," he whispered confidentially. "I invested a lot of time and money going out to learn how to do this right."

She laughed at that. The waiter looked puzzled as she chuckled again when Chance pulled out his reading glasses to order from the menu.

"Dull as dishwater," she whispered under her breath. He shot her a quelling glance, and missed a beat in his wonderfully impressive ordering technique. He opened his mouth to start over again, but instead started to chuckle too. When she laughed along with him, he gave up.

Pointing to the specialty of the house, he simply said, "Give us two of these."

When they were alone again, Chance reached beneath the table and pinched her upper thigh.

"That's for making me screw up. Laughing when you're ordering is like laughing during Communion. I'm sure the chef has been duly informed and is outraged. I'll get you for this, Micah Sinclair. So help me, I will."

"Something tells me, you'd get me anyway."

Chance clucked his tongue. "Whatever happened to that innocent little girl I used to know?"

"She went away," Micah said, the playful tone suddenly gone. "She grew up."

The meal came and was half-consumed when Chance nodded to her empty glass. "Another?" he offered. She nodded and he reached for the remaining champagne settled into the deep frost of the icy silver bucket.

"Thank you." She picked up the glass and took a quick sip trying to block out the thoughts—the horrible, plaguing thoughts she had to share before the night could truly begin. She resented Jonathon intruding on them even in death. She finished the glass quickly and held it out for Chance to refill again.

Micah studied her half-empty plate without really seeing it, then unconsciously began to put the glass to her lips. Chance caught her fingers at the stem before she could lift it.

"We've got a long night ahead of us, Micah. One that's been too long in coming. Let's make it last."

Chance was right, she was on the road to getting smashed. Actually, except for her troubling thoughts, she was feeling quite pleasant. Not quite inebriated. But definitely loose. She welcomed the liberation. It made the tongue a bit thick, but a lot less cautious.

"Want to talk about it?"

She smiled a little nervously. "You see right through me, don't you?"

His hand was in his lap, but she could feel his movement, and then the comforting but exciting sensation of his palm over her knee. Pressing tight.

Micah remained silent. Chance was watching her too intently, and she wondered if instinctively he knew.

The sounds of muted laughter and clinking glasses surrounded them. The distinctive fragrance of delicate French cuisine filling the air.

Micah finished her champagne as Chance watched her drink it.

She wasn't sure, but she thought she heard him say quietly, almost to himself, "Was it *that* bad, *cherie*?"

Once they left and were outside, her spirits lifted. The never-ending party that twilight only enhanced in the French Quarter seemed to dance around them. She almost forgot the earlier heaviness of her thoughts as she gave into the atmosphere. New Orleans at night always reminded her of a high-class call girl wrapped in mink.

Her heels clicked on the pavement, absorbed by the garish, rich texture of coarse laughter, and jazz in the streets. Chance's hand felt wonderfully large and warm. Their tightly laced fingers swayed gently between them.

Turning onto Bourbon Street, Chance stopped at the corner to shrug out of his suit coat, then slung it casually over one shoulder. Nearby, a one-eyed vendor with soiled clothes swayed a bouquet of flowers temptingly toward the crowd.

"Hey, monsieur," he called out when he saw Chance pause. "Flowers for your lady, *oui*?"

Chance fished into his pocket and peeled off a few bills from his money clip.

"Keep the change." He reached for the flowers, then presented them to Micah.

"For the most beautiful rose of them all," he said, sweeping down in a low and gallant bow.

"Oh please, Chance," she groaned.

"Yeah, I know. I never was very good at the sappy stuff." He laughed with her, and caught her around the back of the neck, trailing his fingers up into the short curls of her hair.

"Want to take in a boat ride? The *Natchez* should be taking off around a quarter of ten. Saturdays usually mean a good band."

"That would be perfect. It's been years since I've been on board."

Half an hour later they were on the second deck of the *Steamboat Natchez*. Under the stars. The rhythmic swishing of the paddle wheels set the tempo for the band tuning up. Groups of people called out with jovial spirits; couples snuggled cozily as they looked out at the dark waters beneath. The night was sultry, and the sensual, throbbing sound of the blues began to serenade them from the near distance.

Micah leaned against the railing. Chance moved to brace his hands on either side of her hips, the rail smooth beneath his palms.

He kissed her then. It was a slow, leisurely kiss. And he moved discreetly, so no one would see more than two lovers sharing mouths, and lightly, ever so lightly, cupped her breast within his palm.

The feel of satin slid against her skin and connected with his. She could feel her breast growing fuller, warmer, the tautening of the nipple as he rubbed his thumb in a lazy, slow circle.

The whimper of heightened senses, the aching arousal he was pitching higher, too fast, with nowhere to take them, made her move away.

"Not here," she said. Her voice sounded the way she felt inside—shaky, throaty with desire, a gathering frustration that made her nails bite into her own palms.

"Where?" he said, drawing her closer again. "My house? Yours? We can even stay in the Quarter tonight if you want." He tilted her chin, seeking her eyes in the muted glow of the ship's light. "All I know is . . . I need you. For too long it's been that way with nowhere to take it, except to a substitute. Which is a pretty poor way to spend your life. Wasting it like that."

Now. Tell him now.

"I want to do things to you, Micah . . . all sorts of delicious, wonderful things. I've had a long time to think about tonight, about us. By morning I'm sure you'll rather stay *with* me than away from me . . . tomorrow, the next day, and the one after that."

"Chance . . ."

"Hmmm?"

He nibbled her fingers with tiny, exciting bites. Skimming her palm with his tongue.

She swallowed hard. "Could we dance?"

The clip-clop of the horse echoed through the side streets. The hat with the ears cut out of it bobbed unsteadily on the mare's head, while the driver looked straight ahead, guiding the reins through the familiar route. He paid no heed to the couple nestled in the back. Oblivious to them and caught in his own thoughts, he opened a flask and touched it to his lips.

She leaned back against the warm, cracked leather of the buggy seat. Chance's arm crooked around her shoulders as he pulled her more tightly into his embrace. Moonlight spilled between the gnarled branches of the trees, flitting patterns over the distant worry etching her face.

"I've waited all night, Micah. You've had any number of chances to tell me what's holding you back. I know there's something. And it probably has to do with Jonathon. Let's get it done and over with, because he's not going to come between us when we go to bed. And the night's getting late already."

She couldn't help but stiffen beside him, despite the delicate, soothing motion he made, gliding his fingers through the short, silken bob of her hair.

"Is it so bad, you can't tell even me? Do you really think, knowing where I've been, who I am, that you could say anything that would shock me, or disappoint me?"

She peered into the gathering gloom. Darkness helped. She would talk to the night.

"I'm going to tell you everything, Chance. Don't stop me once I start because I may never find the courage to start again."

He answered her in silence with the reassuring squeeze of her shoulders, while the past waited for her like a gaping abyss.

"You've wondered why I stayed with Jonathon. You've never understood my guilt. But it's all so simple . . . you see, I was part of his sickness. I perpetuated it."

"Micah—"

"No, just let me get on with it." She looked up at the branches reaching toward the sky, trying not to think as she talked. "You weren't the only one who used substitutes. I pretended too. Only the difference was, I was married. To a man who actually loved me. I know what you saw . . . the drinking, the gambling, the other women. But none of that started until . . . I called him by your name in bed."

The branches of midnight darkness passed overhead as she concentrated on their sway, trying to block out the guilt, the black pitch of cloying emotions tainting this night.

"For a long time we tried to pretend it didn't happen. But it did. You were a ghost between us, even from the beginning. I thought you'd never come back when I talked myself into being in love with Jonathon. As for Jonathon, I think he made himself believe that he would eventually be able to make me care for him instead." She shrunk down farther into the seat. "That never happened, of course. Things went from bad to worse."

"But you stayed anyway."

His voice rumbled beneath her ear, a soothing strength she could feel him will to her, helping her to go on.

"Crazy, wasn't it? We saw marriage counselors on several occasions, and for months at a time everything would even seem to be getting better. I would think to myself 'We can *make* this work.'

Stubborn pride. I didn't want to admit defeat. And I felt guilty, of course."

"But you shouldn't have."

She shook her head against his shoulder. "Oh no? A wife whose husband loves her is in love with another man, even calls her husband by his name in bed, shouldn't feel guilty?"

"You can't take that all on yourself, Micah. I was to blame too. Jonathon didn't have to stick around knowing what had happened. We all choose our own courses. We all have to live with our own decisions."

"Jonathon was weak. He couldn't break away. He didn't have the strength. And I lacked the good sense or the guts to make the break for him."

Lord, this hurt, laying the bones bare. And yet, already, she could feel the burden lifting . . . getting lighter as Chance listened to what she had dared tell no one else.

"I'm curious, Micah. Tell me what kind of blackmail he used to keep you with him."

Her head snapped up and her eyes met evenly with his.

"How did you know?"

Chance snorted in disgust. "How? I know you, Micah. You might be loyal to a fault, maybe even have a touch of the martyr bred into you. But you're no masochist. Besides, don't forget I knew Jonathon too. He might have been weak, but he was also manipulative. I can't help but believe he held something over you to keep you there. Especially after he started going down."

She looked away from him. "You're right, Chance, he did manipulate me. But I let him do

it. I think subconsciously it was my self-punish-
ment for wronging him to begin with. He . . . he
said he would kill himself if I ever left him. That
in spite of everything . . . he couldn't live without
me. I know that sounds too farfetched, too dramatic to believe . . . but I believed him. He was
too unstable. I felt I had contributed to his insta-
bility. So I stayed."

Chance's voice was rough, angry. "He wouldn't
have done it, Micah. If he had, it wouldn't have
been your fault. Only his own."

She drew in her breath, then quickly rushed on
before she lost her nerve.

"He did, Chance. I'm sure of it." Her voice suddenly caught. She let Chance move her around
until she sat on his lap, not even wanting to
resist as he tucked her head beneath his chin.

"It's all right, *cherie*. Get it out of your system.
You've been poisoning yourself, keeping it all bot-
tled up."

"Oh, Chance," she sobbed out suddenly. "It was
a nightmare. He came home with cheap perfume
on his clothes, and liquor on his breath. I even
remember seeing lipstick stains smeared on his
throat. I think he did it to make me jealous, to
get back at me for what I had put him through,
for 'castrating his ego' as he used to say. But I
was never jealous, in fact I was glad. I thought
maybe someone else could have him, take the
child off my hands so I wouldn't be responsible
for him anymore. By then I was so tired of it all.
I didn't care anymore. I didn't pity him. I didn't
love him. And I knew that no matter how many
counselors we saw, no matter how many times he

cleaned up his act only to fall again, it would *never* work. Too many years wasted. I was losing my self-respect for staying with it. And for such stupid reasons . . . guilt, pride, fear."

She could feel the gentle sway as he rocked her, and the silence seemed to beg her to go on. The words came now, more easily, spilling freely from their prison.

"When he came staggering into the bedroom that night, I had his clothes packed. I told him he had to leave, that I wanted out. I wanted a divorce. He came at me, yelling that it was all your fault, and my fault, that we were both trash that deserved each other. I hated him then. I hit him . . . the first person I'd ever slapped in my life. He slapped me back. He threw me on the bed—"

The sobs came then, heedless, a torrent as she buried her face against his chest. Chance shushed her, loving her as she cried it out. She was safe, safe at last.

"He tried to rape me, Chance. If I'd had a gun, I would have shot him dead. I fought him, it was all I could do. I scratched his face, I bit him until I drew blood. And, oh, Lord, he wouldn't stop. I thought I was in hell, that I would stay there forever with this madman. He had me down ready to . . . to . . . and then I drew my knee up. Sharp. Hard. And I kicked and kicked until he fell over. Then finally it was over. He was crawling to me and I was backing away, just looking for something to hit him with if he came at me again. He didn't. He just reached into his pocket and threw his money into my face, and told me I could

whore for you the next time. That he was check-
ing out. That I could save myself the divorce fees
because . . . because he'd be dead before I could
file them."

She cried bitterly against his chest now, and
he held her so tightly, she could hardly breathe.
So wonderfully tight against the nightmares.

"He was, Chance. He was dead the next day . . .
he killed himself, I know he did. And I was glad.
I was so happy he was dead. My only fear was
that the insurance company would find out, that
they would take the money away. Little did I know
there wasn't any."

She laughed and cried in a muted hysterical
sob against his shoulder. "And then you came
back. Only I needed my space, I needed to heal
alone. But no matter what, I still felt dirtied. I'm
glad you've kept your distance, Chance. I've
needed that . . . so that I could start to feel clean
again."

"Oh, Lord," he groaned. "Why didn't you tell me
. . . why didn't—" he broke off and clenched her
to him. "You're pure, baby. To me you're pure as
driven snow. And you're not guilty."

Safe in the warm cocoon of his arms, she did
feel pure once more. And the burden was lifted.
Guilt, gone. At last she didn't have to carry the
weight of secrets or shameful sorrows alone.
Chance had given her that. She could tell him
anything, everything, and no matter what, he
would still be there. She was safe. And nothing,
not even that last horrible night with Jonathon,
could touch her. Not ever again.

"Driver," Chance suddenly called out above the

heavy thud of the horse's hooves. "Turn us around."

And then next to her ear he whispered, "We're going home, *ma cherie* . . . home to bury the past."

Eleven

The Lamborghini raced along the now quiet streets of the Garden District. The lush, tropical foliage blended with the stately mansions. The manicured lawns of Saint Augustine grass were deep green and thick from the frequent drizzles of rain or intemperate storms. A breeze was blowing up with the smell of midnight showers on it.

"Micah?"

She turned her face from the fleeting flashes of light through the car window, and let her gaze meet his. Her eyes still felt swollen, red-rimmed. She doubted she made a very pretty sight, her nose was stopped up and was probably red and puffy too.

"I'm okay now, Chance."

He held his hand out between them, wanting to bridge the small distance she had tried to make. She hesitated, took his hand.

"You mean, *we're* okay. Anything that affects you, affects me. Don't pull away from me now,

Micah. I . . . I need you. All of you. I can't stand it when you get that distant look on your face."

"I can't help it, Chance. I feel . . . too exposed. You've seen me at my worst. And I hate to cry. Especially in front of people."

A scowl darkened his features. "But I'm not 'people,' Micah. I'm . . . No, you tell me. Just what *am* I to you?"

She sighed in the darkened interior of the car, the closed space magnifying the sound. Her throat felt scratchy, raw. Her emotions felt the same way.

"I'm not sure, Chance. I get confused about my feelings toward you. You're not an easy man to understand. I never feel that I quite *know* you. I mean, I do know parts of you. But I never know what to expect. One side of you is wonderful, tender, honest, a part I can never get enough of. But just when I think that's who you really are, I catch a glimpse of another side. Something darker, something frightening. You're a very dangerous man inside. And it's dangerous to—" She broke off, unwilling to say more. She knew if she told him she loved him there would be no going back. She could love him in silence. But she wouldn't say the word.

Chance nodded. "I know. But you know me better than anyone else ever has, Micah. And I try, I really do try to be open with you. Only it's not easy to change."

"And will you ever change, Chance? Do you want to?"

"In ways. I've done a lot of things I'm not exactly proud of. But when you're poor . . . well, sometimes a man doesn't have much choice. He either plows his way there, stepping on people in the process, or he ends up staying just where he's at—on the bottom. Now that I'm where I want to be, I have the room to be a little more careful about where I step. I don't want you to have any false illusions about me though, Micah. I'd do it all over again if I had to. I want you to love me. But you need . . . *I* need for you to accept me as I am. I'm flawed, with scars that will never go away. But maybe . . ." he spread his fingers out over the steering wheel, tapping an uneasy tattoo. "Maybe you can find it in your heart to want me anyway."

"I *do* want you, Chance. You know I do."

Chance glanced at her, gave her a piercing look before turning back to the road.

"You *want* me," he said. "Physically, yes. And you thought you loved me when you were a girl. But we're grown-ups now, Micah. With pasts, and traits that are too entrenched to make monumental changes. What I want from you at this stage of life is a lot more than soothing each other's sexual urges. I want your love. Unconditionally. And I want it forever."

Micah could feel the internal quiver. If he only knew he'd had it all along. If he only knew of her fleeting images of their progression in life from now until . . . always. Having children together, building a life, a family, loving each other in old age. She could tell him this now. She could cross the bridge to a permanent commitment. Chance wanted one, he was telling her that in no uncertain terms.

Too much, too soon.

She smiled at him and squeezed his hand.

"Not yet, Chance. But be patient with me. I have no desire for anyone but you."

"Desire," he said quietly. "Well, it's a start. I can build on that." The car came to a sudden stop, and Micah realized they were in front of his house, the engine idling restlessly beneath them. Chance put it in park and turned to her: There was hunger—and more—that she read there. The thrill of the forbidden was suddenly as strong now as it had been when she was a teenager.

In the spare light of the car's illumined dash, she saw the darkening shift of his features, the way they went from the softness of yearning to the purposeful set of stalking, sexual prowess.

Very deliberately, with no pretense of tender embraces melting into some kind of accidental joining, he caught her around the back of the neck and began to rub up and down over the muscles that were stiffening in anticipation. In apprehension.

"Where do we take our 'desires,' Micah?" he said silkily. "Here? The backseat's a little small."

Was there such a thing as getting cold feet and almost shivering with anticipation all at the same time? She wanted to escape this descending cloak of longing; she wanted to cling to it.

She swallowed hard, feeling the difference between them—his comfort of command, her own awkwardness.

"I . . . uh . . . Chance, I'm not very good at this."

He chuckled low in his throat. "Good, I like it

that way." He was treading his fingers up into her hair now, playing with it. "*You* are a very sexy woman, *ma cherie*. Your only problem is, you don't know it."

Was she sexy? She'd never thought of herself that way, certainly not in recent years when she'd felt more like a nursemaid, than a sensual feminine being. She wasn't at all sure she was comfortable with this. Her lips twiched uncertainly, nervousness translating itself into humor.

"Do you find that amusing?"

"No, not really. It's just that . . . I mean," she chuckled softly and met his bemused gaze, "I never exactly thought of myself as a sex kitten before."

"A sex kitten?" Now he chuckled too. "No, I'd never call you that. You're finer, more sophisticated in the sensuality you exude.

"Don't look so surprised, Micah. You think you don't really know me. Sometimes I think there's still a lot of things you don't know about yourself. As a woman, anyway. Would it shock you to know every time you walk into a room I'm affected? It's not something I can control. Believe me, it's happened at the most inopportune times. Like standing in the lobby at the opera."

Micah could feel the heat flush her face—and elsewhere. It was a wonderful boost to know she could do such things to Chance, so effortlessly. And what if she did try to deliberately tempt him? He was looking at her now, watching for a reaction. A shiver went through her.

"I . . . I never noticed." Don't get flustered, she

told herself. Stay calm. She should act as if she talked this way every day.

"No? You never look?"

"Of course not!"

"And I suppose you never fantasize when you're alone . . . about us. About what it would feel like if I touched you here"—he glazed his fingertips over her breast—"*or here.*" Then trailing lower, he drew a slow, intricate pattern over her dress covering the vee of her thighs. "You never think about me making love to you and get hot?"

Micah drew in her breath sharply at the boldness of the action, his directness. It was exciting. Intimidating.

"Why are you talking to me like this?" Her voice was breathy.

"Why?" He lowered his hand to stroke an upward path over the silk of her hose. "Because those are things I've wanted to know for a long time but could never ask. Until now. And besides, I'm giving you your first real lesson in—" his hand stopped, and she could feel the fine tremble between her thighs, and knew that he felt it too. "Why, what have we here? A garter belt? Micah, I'm surprised at you. Pleasantly surprised. Garters can be exciting . . . maybe we'll leave it on tonight." He flipped the catch easily, and she could feel the silk slither downward as her eyes grew wide in the dark. "But then again, maybe we won't."

What in heaven's name was she doing here? All hot and cold and scared to death all of a sudden. He was too worldly. She was too . . . unprepared for this kind of finesse.

"Chance, you're—"

"I'm what? Naughty? You mean you didn't know? Bad boys only get worse with age. Or maybe they just have a natural aptitude for developing their baser instincts. I know how I like it. Don't you want to find out? Aren't you just aching to know?"

"Please, don't," she said, barely managing to get the words out.

"Please, don't what? Talk about it? Be honest with you? If you want pretty words and a pretense of sweetness to lure you into bed, that's not me. I want you, Micah. And I love you. But don't expect me to be a gentleman. In public, yes. In bed? Forget it. You're nearly thirty, and I doubt you know any more about sex than you did when we were kids. Now it's time you learned what grown-ups do in the dark . . . or the light. If you're not ready for this, tell me now. But I thought you wanted it as much as I did. If I thought wrong, I'll take you home this minute. This has to be right for both of us, or it won't be right at all."

His hand slid back down her thigh, raising the flesh with it. He reached for her chin then, turning her to him.

He loves me. He cares. She was thrilled to hear those words. She'd known all along, but *hearing* him say it. *He loved her.* Words he had never said before. And she was sure, never to another woman. Words that made her melt.

"Would you be angry with me?"

"Angry? Not exactly that. Just frustrated. *Very* frustrated."

"And . . . what do you do when you're frustrated? I . . . I know I have no right to ask, Chance. But do you . . . go to . . ." She couldn't say it. She really had no right, not if she was turning him away.

"No. I don't. The fast girls are gone. I haven't slept with another woman since the day you were widowed. I might have . . . uncivilized tendencies, but that doesn't mean I don't have principles. Or emotional commitments that are more important to me than slaking an appetite."

When she didn't answer him, he put the car into gear and began to press his foot to the accelerator. She wasn't sure if what she was doing was right or wrong. But instinctively she reached out and turned off the ignition.

Silence. No running motor in the background. No nearby traffic. And no words. Only the sound of their breathing: His deep and expectant, hers shallow and quickened. The decision had been made. There was no taking it back.

"You're sure?" He peered at her through the dark.

She nodded.

"Say it."

"I'm sure." Her voice was shaking. "I want you to make love to me . . . just as you are."

The hardness behind his eyes was gone, given way to a glimmer . . . of delight, of warmth.

"Stay there." He got out and came around to her door, causing her to gasp in surprise as he caught her up under the legs and swung her into his arms.

She laughed with a sudden and unexplainable

abandon as he dramatically kicked the door shut with his foot.

"You're a crazy man, Chance Renault."

"And you're crazy about me, aren't you?"

She gave into the impulse to nuzzle the side of his neck with her nose, inhaling his deliciously masculine scent. "Mmmm."

Chance stopped in midstride. He made a motion as though he meant to drop her.

"Chance!" she yelped, hanging tight to keep her balance.

"Say you're crazy about me," he insisted, nipping the lobe of her ear.

"Yes!" She laughed helplessly as he goosed her ribs.

"Yes, what?" He goosed her again.

"Yes! Oh . . . oh, Uncle! . . . Yes, I'm crazy about you!"

He picked up his pace and headed for the house. "I've *never* been your uncle, and I've got no intentions of starting now. In fact, we're about to enact one of those fantasies I was telling you about. It's the one where I sweep you off your feet and carry you up to my bedroom for the first time. By the way, you're supposed to gasp in awe at your surroundings."

By now he had opened the door to the house she had driven by so many times wondering how it would look inside and what kind of creature comforts a man like Chance would surround himself with.

He was still holding her, looking at her expectantly, while she took in the surroundings he was obviously so proud of.

"Chance, it's beautiful."

And it was. The rooms had high ceilings, huge spaces, leather and chintz, antiques and contemporary. From the kitchen to the library, from the drawing room to the game room, the house was exquisite.

"I'm proud of my house. When I bought the place, I thought it looked like home. Except it was too empty. Still is. . . . It means a lot to me that you like it here."

They were on the top landing of the stairs, and there was no doubt in her mind where he was taking her next. Four doors faced the balustrade. Chance strode to one, shifting her weight in his arms as he reached for the handle. The door opened, and she mentally readied herself to confront the bedroom.

Blues and greens and yellows and pinks splashed gaily around the room. From the wallpaper to the platform rocker. From the chest of drawers to the big stuffed giraffe. From the teddy bear mobile to the baby bed.

A nursery!

"No one comes in here. Just me. Sometimes I sit in the rocker and I dream. About the way I wished life had turned out. About the children we never had. The children we were. It's a little strange, I know. But the nursery was here when I bought the house, and the house always seemed so big, and this room seemed especially empty. I don't know what possessed me to do it, but one day I just decided I wanted to fill the nursery up. There weren't any kids. Hell, there was no one but me. But it was a whim. One I gave in to. And—why are you looking at me like that?"

Micah could only shake her head in disbelief. "You, Chance . . . you never stop amazing me."

"Oh? You never thought I might have paternal instincts? That maybe I've felt I was missing something in life, or that I wanted more than money and power?"

"Well . . . something like that. I just never really thought about you wanting children. That's all." The way he was looking at her, she knew he had wanted more and was disappointed. "At least, not until recently," she confessed at last.

"I've thought of you being a mother," he said hastily. "What a good one you'd make. I always wondered why you didn't have any. Lord knows, if you had, it wouldn't make any difference in my feelings for you now, and I'd love your children just because they were yours. But I'm selfish. I wanted you to have mine . . . if you can have them."

Children. Chance wanted to talk about having children, implying a long future, when she'd been expecting a simple seduction. He was swinging into all the nooks and crannies of her hopes and fears with the quick ease of a trapeze artist. It left her a little breathless. More vulnerable to him than ever before.

"I can have them. He couldn't."

Chance nodded slowly. "I'm glad it wasn't you. Do you know how many times I've pictured you in that rocker, nursing a baby at your breast? I think about it, I remember what your breasts looked like when we were young."

"You remember?"

"I remember everything. I remember the way you tasted. Your shape, the way your breasts fit in my hands. Only you're fuller now." As he spoke his hand found her breasts. Over the silk of her dress he caressed her, making the mound even fuller. She could feel the quickening inside: In her bosom and the aching core between her thighs. She sought his mouth, wanting him, his taste, to urge him suddenly on.

When they pulled away to catch their breath, Micah whispered next to his ear, "I think it's time you showed me the rest of the house."

In his room, he turned on music. The blues. The heavy thud of sensuality pulsed to the beat of their intimate rhythm, while the low rumble of thunder shook the night. He undressed her to the music, to the thunder, stripping the last threads of civilization away. She savored the feel of his hands, the way they moved confidently, yet almost reverently against her skin.

The dress was shed, slowly, deliberately. She wore only the silk chemise, her lacy slip, stockings held up by the garter belt, minus one catch. Chance stepped away from her then, the wispy glow of scented candles illumining them, making this space more intimate than just darkness.

"Don't cross your arms," he whispered gruffly.

She made herself stand still, pliant, letting him look at her, trying to get his fill. She could feel the remnants of self-consciousness, but his eyes were warm and appreciative. And intoxicating. Far more heady than the wine he'd just poured. He handed her the glass as she stood there feeling more naked than dressed.

Chance tilted the glass toward her lips. She drank as he urged her to, not too much, enough to dull what little fear was left. Fear of this heavy sensuality, this unknown entry to a place she had only glimpsed before.

She reached for him, and he complied. Giving her a taste, teasing her as he stepped away, taking the glass with him, laying it aside with his own next to the bed—the big four-poster, intricately carved, heavy, and very masculine.

"Turn," he commanded, circling once with his hand.

She could feel her feet slowly begin to move. Her brain felt numb but acute with awareness. A tingle was spreading. A frightening sensation, some of her control being taken away; but too exciting to resist.

Micah made the circle, feeling his eyes hot, intense, intimately upon her. Seeing the lust, the need, the love etched clearly on his face as his gaze caught hers in the cheval glass, old and beveled, positioned behind her.

Something sacred and immutable passed between them before she dared a fleeting glance at her own body in the mirror. As before, he signaled, and she began to move again, arousing him deliberately, and consequently, herself.

Gracefully she turned until they faced again.

"Take it off."

Her hand lifted slowly. A part of her, and yet, detached. She shut out the far cry of fearfulness, of any hesitance that was left.

The chemise strap fell down in a diagonal curve, invitingly coy upon her arm. Her breasts, heavy and full as they strained against the silk, felt the fabric's caress riding upon the peaks.

Her hands began to work the tiny buttons. She

didn't look down to see what she was doing. Instead, her eyes sought his approval . . . as he watched her. As she gave in to the temptation of watching the strain of his pants.

The chemise undone, her breasts were still covered. A small shrug. The chemise fell off, creating a puddle of silk beside her stockinged feet. She paused, and waited, letting him look. His gaze rose and met hers. For long moments they sought the secrets of hearts meeting there. Too many years, they seemed to say. Too many nights dreaming of this, wanting so urgently, afraid never to have.

He gave a small nod. And she went on.

The pale slip pooled beside the matching top, and she stood with her shoulders held proudly, with elegance. Offering herself, all that she was, only to him.

He nodded his approval.

"Well done, *ma cherie*. As you can see, I approve."

She could feel herself flush, the rise of blood in her veins, as she whispered, "I lied. I do look at your pants sometimes. Wanting to see you react like this."

He smiled. "I know." He came toward her, walking with purpose. "You can stop now. I want to finish the rest for you."

He crossed over to where she stood by the bed. For a while he simply looked, gazing at her nudity from behind in the mirror. Then his hand came up, brushing lover's caresses down her spine before falling lower, lower still. Lifting the delicate catch, he released the fabric of French silk hose.

He worked his way down, lowering the stockings, removing them from her feet. Touching, soothing, he seemed mesmerized by the lift of her foot, its shape and texture.

"I'm a leg man, you know." He kissed the tops of her feet, then ascended with soft kisses climbing the length of her legs. As the wisp of her garter belt fell away, his attention shifted.

"I'm also a man who goes for nicely shaped behinds." His fingertips traced the contour of each cheek, separately, then as a whole. Micah could feel herself getting cold and then hot, and then it was too hard to even breathe. Her legs nearly buckled as he traced his nose against her, and then his lips. Though he didn't touch the hidden ache buried within her folds.

With one hand he reached up and expertly began to fondle a breast. "But I like breasts even more." He murmured it against her belly, vibrating the sensitive skin beneath.

She was completely naked, and his clothes were all too intact. She urged him upward.

"Chance, please."

"Please what? Touch you, kiss you? Stroke you *there*?"

The quick slice of his fingertips skimmed over the sheen of her femininity. And then her legs did give way. She fell against him, and he caught her firmly, anchoring his mouth between her thighs. She was helpless, caught there against his merciless probing.

It was too wonderful to bear. A delicious agony. No. It couldn't be happening. Not this quickly.

She tried pushing him away, pulling at him to

stop, to rise to her at once. In silence, in the fleet movement of his tongue, his low growl of warning, he denied her. He denied her the right to ever say no to his wanting again. He denied her the right to control her own longing, pushing her closer, closer, until she plunged off the edge.

She was crying. She could feel the tears of release pouring out of her. Could hear the keening wail of his name fall from her lips. And the floor was suddenly beneath her back, and he was moving inside her with the rush of his fingers, the vibration of his hand. He was talking to her without words, making sounds that were guttural and inarticulate. Or maybe she was too far gone to understand.

She thought she must have fainted. His lips were beside her ear, calling her name. Saying he loved her, and now she was his. Would always be his. She felt herself being lifted in his arms, weightless, her head falling back, still spinning in electrical arcs.

"See me, Micah. Look at me now." She opened her eyes, coming slowly back to reality. He stood there, naked and proud. His physique was tough, hard, nothing soft or immature about it. A man of rough, coarse hair, with muscles that were heavy and thick. Not pretty in the least. But how very manly he was, how eloquently strong.

She found the strength to lift her arms, asking him in.

He came to her, laying by her side at first. Gently, so surprisingly tender, he traced the shapes and curves beneath his fingers, learning her in repose, even while the heat anchored in his body pressed impatiently into her hip.

"Chance," she whispered, reaching for him, touching him. In a fluid, swift motion, he was over her. His chest pressed into hers, then lifted. Just high enough so he could stroke her breasts, dip, and touch his mouth to them by turns.

The edge of passion that he had stoked then soothed had begun to mount again. Nothing had ever approached the magnitude of this. No, not even the night when they had lain naked and all too young.

The aching began again; the deepness burned within her. She craved to hold him closer. That close to her heart, that much a part of her.

"I want you inside me," she whispered. No, she had never said those words before. How easy they were to say now, how natural. She pulled him over her with a sudden, urgent strength. "Please, Chance."

She reached for him to guide him within. He caught her hand.

"No, not like that." His fingers slipped through hers. *"Together."*

He slid inside, their clasped hands leading him home. So full. So warm. So incredibly right. How had she lived without this? She never could, never again.

"From now on, Micah," he whispered, looking down into her face, *"always,* together."

Just short of his ultimate destiny, he stopped. She let him take her hands. He spread them wide in surrender as he held them firmly apart upon the bed.

The texture of crisp cotton rubbed against her back. The rough hair of his chest played across the smoothness of her breasts. The beginnings of his heavy beard scratched a light burn over the skin of her cheeks, the delicious rawness of her chin. But it was the feel inside, the internal holding that pinned her, bound her to him, and beneath him.

She wound her legs around the backs of his, silently pleading for the rest. She raised her hips up in entreaty. He fixed her with a satisfied, meaningful pout, and made a small retreat.

"Love me, Micah."

"I do," she cried.

"Say it." His breathing was growing harsher; his thrusts harsher too.

"I love you. Oh, Lord, Chance. I could never stop loving you."

"I'm going to marry you, Micah Sinclair. And you're going to have our children. Our future starts tonight."

Faster. Harder.

"Please, Chance. Come in me. *Now . . . please now.*"

He filled her then, spending himself into her womb.

Time expanded, contracted with only the rain and the walls to listen as they whispered their intimate vows. Still buried inside he grew large again . . . and yet again.

They had forever. They had each other. They had now.

Micah stretched languorously. Preparing for the evening had been quite an unnerving experience, she'd wanted to look just right. But now, rumpled, sated, her hair mussed and her makeup smudged, she felt as though she must look at least a hundred times better. The night of loving had brought them closer in a way nothing else ever could have.

"How do you feel?"

She laughed a sensuous sound, pleased with herself, her nudity. The ache of too much satiation between her thighs.

They snuggled and whispered intimacies and made the sounds of morning lovers.

"I'll be right back." She nipped his shoulder playfully then bounded off the bed.

"You'd better be, or I'm liable to come looking for you. If I have to get out of bed, there's a penalty attached, of course."

"Oh?" she teased, deliberately wriggling her rear end as she sauntered toward the door. "What if I want to stop in the kitchen and make some coffee?"

"Coffee? Hmmm. Maybe I could grant you a pardon if there's coffee involved."

Micah stopped beside the dresser. Turning to Chance, the sensuous woman retreated a bit back to the discreet woman of the day before.

"Do you have something I could wear around? I feel a little awkward walking through your house stark naked."

"Okay, just so you don't make it a habit. I find that I definitely prefer you naked. Look in the dresser. The T-shirts are under the—"

Reaching deep into the drawer, Micah's fingers contacted the cotton cloth beneath a stack of briefs. She pulled it out, with a strange surge of proprietary excitement at wearing one of Chance's underthings against her skin.

A folded sheet of paper that had apparently been wedged at the bottom caught under her fingers as she lifted the shirt. She couldn't help but be curious about what Chance had obviously meant to hide in there, knowing the lingerie drawer was where she kept most of her own personal letters or cards. But it wasn't polite to pry.

Glancing at the folded paper as she moved to put it back, she stopped. Dead. This paper was familiar. A too terribly familiar sheet of ivory with a scroll of raised letterhead at the top. Someone's personal stationery.

She felt as though her stomach had just been brutally jabbed with a sharp elbow. In the distance she could hear Chance's voice, sounding urgent.

"Wait a minute, Micah . . . don't look in . . . here let me get that."

He was throwing the covers back, rising naked from the bed, as she turned to him slowly, in what surely was a nightmare she would be waking up from any minute.

In the nightmare she didn't try to hide the stricken look that was etched in bold relief across her face, or the stinging tears she couldn't stop from flowing in shimmering streams from her accusing eyes.

His face was ashen, nearly as stricken as hers felt as he came to her. She jerked away the moment he touched her arm, the exact same moment the note fell from her nerveless fingers and sailed blindly to the floor. The IOU lay there between them, sharp as a razor blade, slashing her trust in two.

Twelve

They stood facing each other. Naked. Too vulnerably naked in the cold, startling light of day.

Once his body demanded he breathe again, Chance could hear the tight, rasping sound. It sounded loudly disproportionate between his ears. This couldn't be happening. Not after all he'd gone through, waiting, hoping. He couldn't bear to lose her again. Not now, not after knowing what it meant to hold her again, filling up the gaping, empty void that life had been without her.

"Micah. Listen to me. Please—" He reached for her hands. Needing something, anything, of substance, to assure himself she was still there.

She eluded his grasp as though he were poisonous.

"How *could* you, Chance? You made me believe in you. That you were being honest with me, that I was doing something *all on my own*. You knew how important that was to me! You knew—" She snorted with disgust, the anger and hurt too entwined for him to separate. "You couldn't have let me down more, Chance. Not even if you planned it."

She was waiting, looking at him anxiously. She wanted an answer, something to explain away the obvious, because she was being torn up inside too. He could lie, tell her some glib excuse she might be all too ready to accept rather than the awful truth.

He braced himself, the armor of self-protection slipping for once, just when he needed it the most.

"You were never meant to see that, Micah."

"I suppose not. After all, you wouldn't want me to know you were just as guilty of gambling as Jonathon. That you were no better than him—"

"That's enough! Call me anything vile you can think of. But don't you *dare* ever compare the two of us again." The anger felt good, familiar. It muted the horrible feeling of vulnerability threatening to overwhelm him.

"No? Then you tell me what's the difference. You gambled with him. *Him* of all people—"

"That's right. Him, of *all* people. Tell me something, Micah. How else was I supposed to learn how you were doing, get some kind of idea as to how fast your marriage was going down the tubes? What was I going to do? Call you? Say 'Hey, babe, how's tricks? Got a divorce on the agenda anytime soon? Let me know when it's final and we'll tie the knot as soon as you're free.' " He ran a hand through his rumpled hair in agitation. He hated the way she just kept staring at him: Wide-eyed, hurt, and distant. If only she'd say something, anything. The silence was too accusing.

"In a way, I'm glad you know that I played poker with him. You probably would have found out eventually . . . only I wish I'd been able to tell you in my own time."

"Your own time? And when would that have been, Chance? Ten years, twenty? Maybe just a note you could leave for me after you were dead too?"

He shook his head, not really sure of the answer himself. "When I felt our relationship was strong enough to handle it. Please, Micah, try to understand. The way I saw it, that was my one link with you. Twisted as it was, *ma cherie.*"

"Don't call me that," she snapped.

For a moment he wasn't sure if she was going to slap him or scream at him. Maybe fall on the floor and sob. Or worst of all, just turn around and leave. Her chest was heaving, making her breasts pout temptingly. The morning air, the stimulation of fury was causing her nipples to contract, and he remembered all too vividly his mouth suckling her there what now seemed so long ago.

Before he could stop himself, his eyes traced the defiant stance she presented. His own body reacted to the challenge, the knowledge of her hidden secrets, and the power he possessed in making her yield. He longed to make her yield now, spending their anger in a heated frenzy rather than in the lonely isolation of words and more words—hurtful things that could never be taken back.

"You're disgusting," she said. "How can you stand there looking at me so hungrily, after something like this?" She began to yank on her own clothes, so sensuously discarded the night before. "Get dressed, would you?"

He was tempted to keep them off, just to unnerve her. Remind her of their night together. Only the important thing now was to undo the damage, to somehow put it right again. Antagonizing Micah would only defeat that purpose. Scowling, he reached into the bottom drawer and got out a pair of faded jeans.

He noticed Micah kept her eyes averted. Just past his shoulder. He moved so that she had to meet his eyes, so that she could see how deeply he hurt for her, how very much she meant to him.

"I love you, Micah." He bent down swiftly and retrieved the paper, held it up between them. "See this? It's nothing. Let it go. What we've got between us is too good, too right. And Jonathon's not going to take that from us again."

Very deliberately he tore the paper, the sound of it rending the silence of the room. It was now in halves, then quarters. He tore and tore until there was nothing but shreds. Then he turned his hand upside down and let them fall, littering the small space between them, floating on the gulf that he was trying desperately to bridge.

Sadly Micah shook her head. "Do you actually think it's that easy, Chance? That by tearing the evidence up, it doesn't exist? No. It's still there between us. Even now my mind's firing questions, demanding to know things I'm afraid to ask. Things that are bound to point out just how different we really are."

He took a step forward, but Micah stuck her hand out, stopping him. "Don't touch me now. All it can do is confuse me. I want some answers, Chance. Honest ones . . . if you're even capable of it."

"I'll give you any answers you want or need. Honest ones, Micah. Because nothing is worth your distrust, no matter how unsavory the answer might be."

The hurt tightened around his heart. As long as he could remember, she could tear him apart with no more than her distance; and her distrust of him now was painfully bitter. Chance clenched his jaw, enduring it.

She hesitated, watching his face, as though searching for anything sly or dishonest there. She finally gave a short, curt nod of the head.

"Did you play with him often?" The words came out faint, the dread in knowing too obvious for him to miss.

"Often enough." There was no reaction except a tight swallowing motion. She was waiting for more, her silence told him that. "About once a month . . . for the last two years or so."

She closed her eyes, as though trying to block out the damning truth.

"Then this isn't the only one?"

He shook his head slowly. He braced himself, knowing what would come next.

"How many?"

"About a dozen."

She made a noise. A strangled, sobbing catch in the throat. Instinctively he stepped closer.

She shook her head in a short, stilted motion. "No," she said quickly. "Stay back."

He understood, and nodded, feeling a crumbling sensation inside, afraid to confront the growing, terrible premonition.

"How much?"

"Micah, you don't want to—"

"I said, how much, damn you!"

Get it done with . . . and tell her no lies.

"Thirteen grand. Give or take a few hundred."

"He owed you that much and you kept playing with him?" She looked stunned, her eyes wide and disbelieving. "You knew he'd never pay up. What were you going to do with your collection of IOUs, Chance? Paper your office with them?"

"Buy your freedom."

Her mouth gaped open. She shook her head once, twice, as though she were trying to wake up from a bad dream. What was he thinking in telling her this? He'd vowed the truth, but this was better left unsaid.

"My *what*?"

"Forget it, Micah. Ask me something else."

"You were going to *buy my freedom*?" She seemed hung there, unable to get past the fatal revelation.

"It was killing me, Micah," he said urgently, desperate to make her understand. "Seeing the way you were sinking deeper, the way he was pulling you down with him. Especially after you refused to leave, I had to think of some way, some plan to get you out of there. . . . I decided if Jonathon owed me enough money, he'd be willing to make a trade. My silence and forgiveness of his debts to me in exchange for him letting you go."

"But that's blackmail!"

"Hell, no, lady! That's desperation! For the love of heaven, Micah, I was doing it for you. Everything's been for you."

"Well I don't want it." She shuddered, her face etched in distaste. "You've built your empire by stepping on people, being mean and dirty, and I want nothing of it. I've made excuses for you, Chance, always. But no more. It was bad enough that you were a cutthroat in your business dealings, but this takes the cake." She pressed her hand over her heart as though she were covering the hurt. Her voice came out choked. "You tried to buy me."

"No!" He was losing her, losing everything he'd ever wanted. He had to get her back. The desperation was eating him alive, crawling through his insides, shooting streaks of black behind his eyes.

"No," he repeated. His hands clenched by his sides as he forced himself not to grab her to him until he felt safe, sure that she was still his. "Listen to me, Micah. No one could ever buy you. Because no one owns you but yourself. I just wanted your freedom. Once he let you go, the rest was up to you. I had no guarantee that you'd come back to me. Only hopes and dreams that refused to die, that I kept clinging to when there was nothing else to keep me going. At least this way I had a chance. It was all I had."

She seemed to slump with the heaviness of the confession.

"That paper was meant to be your ticket out. But that was between me and Jonathon. What's on the floor has nothing to do with you."

"Maybe not. But it has everything to do with *us*." She raised her head slowly. "One reason I could give myself to you was because I felt I had finally started to come into my own. That I had proven to myself, and to you, that I could stand on my own two feet."

"What are you talking about? You *have* taken care of yourself."

"Have I? You knew from the very beginning how important it was to me that I invested *my* money. Not yours. And that's exactly what our little 'partnership' is. Yours, all yours. Because even with my paltry investment, I still owe you."

"Dammit, Micah," he growled. For once in his life he'd wanted to help someone, and all she could do was throw it in his face. "Sometimes I get just a little sick of your pride, you know that? You can't see beyond it. Money has nothing to do with us. If you'd rise above this constant need to keep proving whatever the hell it is you're trying to prove to yourself, you'd see what you've really accomplished."

She took a step back. He matched it with a step forward, then relentlessly forged ahead, trying to make her see reason.

"Do you realize that you've painted nearly a whole house? Wallpapered it? Fixed plumbing, and turned the yard from an eyesore into a selling point? You have real talent—an eye. By the time you finish—"

"I'm not."

The room went deathly quiet.

"I beg your pardon?" He said it slowly, making sure she caught the edge of warning there.

"I *said* . . . I'm not finishing. I'm going to have my lawyer turn over my share of the property to you. And I'm going to do it today."

She turned as if to leave. His hands snaked out. Taking her by the shoulders, he snapped her around to face him.

"Oh no, you're not," he said.

"Oh yes. I *am*."

His hands tightened and he fought the urge to shake some sense into her. "My patience is wearing thin, Micah, so get this straight. You are legally bound as my partner, like it or not. When I had my lawyer draw up our agreement, I made sure it was airtight, and there's no way you're getting out of it. You're going to finish that house, come hell or high water."

"Like hell I will. It's yours, Chance. Just count my labor and down payment toward the outstanding balance. Send me a bill for the rest. I'll make sure you get your money before anyone else does."

He had to make her stick it out; it was the only way to keep her close until they solved this.

He measured each word carefully, spooning the acid to bite. "You disappoint me, Micah. I never had you pegged for a quitter. After all, quitters are cowards. The yellow streak sticks to their backs like neon. You can see it a mile away, every time they run. That's something I've never understood—how quitters must figure it's easier to walk than to confront the problem head-on."

She flinched. He smiled mirthlessly, detesting the cruelty of what he had no choice but to do. Chance went on, forcing his voice to sound businesslike and impersonal.

"See, Micah, what we've got is a problem with direction here. If you decided to stay and work things out instead of running, you should have the balance worked off by the time we sell the house. And have a profit to show." He shrugged with supreme indifference. "However, if you do decide to quit, you'll still have the entire balance to settle with me. You would have worked free of charge, and your down payment would be mine, too, of course. By default, Micah. Think about it. That's an awfully high price to pay for a load of false pride."

Something was going on behind her eyes . . . it was hard to tell what. An assessment, some kind of mental gymnastics as she came to grips with reality. Common sense and incredulity and hurt pride warring within her.

"All right," she said quietly, slowly.

He gave a curt nod. "You'll make a shrewd businesswoman yet, Micah. The cardinal rule is . . . never let emotions interfere with a sound decision."

"So I'm learning from the master. All the more reason to leave any kind of emotion out of our business . . . and that is all we're dealing with here. Business. I'll keep my end of the bargain, you just stay out of my way."

"If that's the way you want it."

His eyes searched hers, before she took a deep breath and looked away. He knew she still felt enough for him to hurt, the pain in her too obvious for him to miss.

"That's the way I want it."

His hands were still on her shoulders, no longer clenching in anger, but soft with regret, and the need to harbor what tenderness he could before she pulled away.

Micah seemed to be savoring it, too, and then with a determined look she shrugged them away. Reaching behind her ears, she unlatched the emeralds that he knew had been her grandmother's—the ones that enticed him even now to press his lips against the sweetness of her neck.

She reached for his hand, and drew it between them, palm up. He felt the emeralds fall lightly in the center.

"Micah, please—"

"No." She shook her head. "Those are worth at least the balance, Chance. Keep them until we sell . . . just consider it collateral."

He reached for her. She shrugged his touch away. Stiffly she got herself together, and without another word, strode to the door.

"Wait," he called out. "Let me drive you home."

She paused there, her hand grasping the frame. "I need to be alone, Chance. I . . . want to walk awhile. When I get tired, I'll catch a cab. Don't worry about me."

Even with the distance between them, he could see her unsteady hold, the way she trembled. She turned just enough that their gazes met.

There were volumes spoken in that small silence. They shared a common pain, an unlikely affinity in this moment—the confusion of how things had gone so wrong.

"How *could* you, Chance?" she whispered suddenly through the falling of her tears. "Can you even imagine what this does to me?"

He nodded, knowing too well. Her gaze shied away from his, as though even looking at him was too incisive, the cut too fresh to endure it.

"I know it's too soon," he said quietly, around the unbidden constriction of his throat. "But when you can start seeing past your own pain, just try to remember that I'm hurting too."

He wasn't sure, but thought she gave a small, hesitant nod. As she walked away his feet moved compulsively to the door to watch her as long as he could. Then she was gone, and there wasn't a damn thing he could do about it. He wanted to curse, he wanted to go after her and force the earrings back where they belonged. Even more, he wanted to lay her down and take her to a place where none of this torment existed, where lips soothed, and bodies forgot.

Chance opened his palm and looked down at the emeralds. He remembered the night on the porch when he had first touched them, the kisses, the hunger. Then he remembered the fleeting glance that had passed between them as she had taken them off moments ago.

Despite her words, despite it all, it was a glance that he clung to now as he let that final parting mingle with his despair. He grasped the emeralds tight, and shut his eyes, taking his only comfort in the unspoken message:

She might not like him, she might not trust him. But, thank Heaven, she couldn't stop loving him.

Thirteen

Chance listened to the reverberation of the engine, trying to block out the pounding between his temples. Drumming his fingers on the dash released some of the pent-up energy that had been building over the past few weeks.

He had known better than to even try the flowers routine again, sure that would only anger her more. And anger was mostly what was left now; the pain and shock had dulled to a bearable level. Only the anger hadn't died—if anything, it had just kept building in the face of her silence.

He was learning to hate the silence, the solitude. He hated it almost as much as that brusque, impersonal voice she used with him now.

He was emotionally drained, mentally exhausted, and frustrated. As if that wasn't enough to try his patience to the limit, the added pressure of the interested buyer had managed to tip the scales.

Chance stopped drumming his fingers. He

clenched his jaw. He knew she was in the house since her car was parked in the driveway.

"Enough," he said to himself. "We're getting this straight, once and for all. I can't stand another minute of this."

Just in case she decided to retreat again, he backed up and blocked her car as he had that day that seemed like months ago now. He felt better already. They could yell, they could scream, accuse and defend, in fact, he hoped they did, because at least that would be some kind of communication, and anything would be better than this never-ending stalemate. He'd take wrath over indifference any day.

He got out of the car and slammed the door behind him, itching for a fight, anything that might lead to a reconciliation.

Noticing what a beautiful job she'd done with the yard's landscaping, his grimace softened. He'd be the first to admit he was basically pretty selfish, and that extended to keeping Micah as a business partner. She had a good eye for color and design. This house might be gone soon, but they had a good thing going businesswise, and he wasn't about to give that up anymore than anything else he counted as his.

Shutting the door behind him, he turned and latched it. Things were going to heat up around here before they cooled down, and he wasn't about to have anyone intrude at a bad time.

The woven gray carpeting helped muffle his approach. Chance found her in one of the bedrooms. He stood quietly by the door frame and watched. She didn't realize he was there. Hopefully she was too absorbed with the curtains she was hanging to notice for a while longer.

She cursed softly to herself as one of the hooks missed and two more came undone. He smiled and swallowed the urge to tease her about it—not much, just enough to ruffle her feathers and make the blood rush to her cheeks.

Lord, did he love the woman. He'd tried to tell her that a dozen times since she'd found the chit, but she'd let him know it wasn't what she wanted to hear. *Women.* What did she want from him anyway? A promise never to gamble again? Well hell, that was no big deal, in fact he'd already promised her that. She'd met his promise with silence.

Stubborn, that's what she was. Stubborn and beautiful, and even now he could feel the ache begin. He'd gone without for too long—without her affection, without her company. He was missing the hell out of her.

"No more," he said in a low growl.

Micah jerked around at the sound of his voice. The last hook caught and the drape fell neatly in place.

She fought the urge to draw the drapes away from the window. Somehow with them closed, the room seemed too closed in, too intimate. She could see the way he was clenching and unclenching his fists, the darkened cast to his face.

Chance wanted a fight. No question about it.

Micah's jaw clenched to match his. If that's what he wanted, well, she just might be inclined to give him one.

Micah got off the stepladder and put her hands on her hips, ready to face off.

"No more what?"

"No more shutting me out. That's what. I've tried to give you time to get over things, Micah. But my patience is gone. I screwed up, okay? I admit it. Be mad at me if you have to, stay mad at me. But the least you can do is talk about it."

"About what? About the way I feel like slugging you for trying to run my life? I still can't believe you, Chance. Imagine, gambling to barter for *my* divorce."

"I *told* you, Micah. *I'm sorry.* What's done is done and I can't reverse it. Now get off your high horse because I'm through apologizing. It's time we moved on."

He pushed away from the door, and she had more than a premonition of what Chance had on his mind. He not only wanted a fight, he wanted *her.*

"Go away, Chance. I'm not ready to 'move on.' "

His brows drew together ominously. The stool was touching her ankles and she took a side step back, putting it in front of her instead, as though it were a barrier he couldn't cross.

Chance stopped in front of the stool. Without taking his eyes from hers, he kicked it aside. She couldn't help but cringe inwardly, feeling the gathering storm whip up around them. Even the air seemed to crackle with the volatile energy of opposing forces.

"Did it ever occur to you that maybe I have feelings too? I'm tired of you rejecting all my attempts to mend the broken bridges. But most of all I'm tired of making the only effort around here to work things out. A relationship takes two, Micah, and you've got to meet me halfway. You've had plenty of time to lick your wounds. Now it's time to kiss and make up."

The gall of him! Did he actually think he could just ask for an apology after what he'd done? Kiss and make up, indeed.

"Do you know what infuriates me more than anything?" she said. "It's that I don't even think what you did bothers you, or that you even believe it was wrong. You're just sorry I found out." A muscle jumped tensely beside his jaw, and it made the coiling in the pit of her stomach even tighter.

"Am I right, or not?" she challenged hotly.

"When are you going to quit expecting the world to play by your rules, Micah? Of course I'm not sorry for what I did. But isn't it enough that I feel badly for the pain it caused you? Gambling means nothing to me. If I never see another card again, fine. But if you want me to put on an act and pretend I regret my actions, you're out of luck. That would be a lie. I've promised myself there won't be any lies to come between us. And as far as I'm concerned, that's a hell of a lot more important than mourning something that happened a long time ago. It's over. Done with. Now let it go."

She had known from the very beginning what kind of man he was. And what did she expect, that he was going to magically become Mr. Goody-two-shoes just because she'd slept with him?

Admitted her love for him? He'd told her from the beginning not to expect miracles, but she had.

Micah sighed heavily. "You know, Chance, sometimes I can't help but wish you could change just a little. Show some kind of remorse for running roughshod over people. If you did, maybe I wouldn't feel so intimidated by it all, or threatened that you'll try to dominate me too."

"And sometimes I wish you could just loosen up and quit trying to fit life into such tidy little compartments. Everything's so black-and-white with you, Micah. The real world has lots of shades of gray. I find myself trying to live up to your expectations at times, and, lady, that's a mighty tall order to fill. In the end we just have to be able to live with ourselves, and the decisions we make, whether they turn out to be right or wrong. Now how about it? A truce? I'm not asking for the stars, I just want a second chance."

Suddenly she felt so weary of it all. She was too tired to fight.

"All right," she agreed slowly. "We'll try one more time. I think we both deserve that much. But we'll wait until we've sold the property."

Fourteen

"Okay, Micah, here's your cut. Twenty grand. Not bad for a three-thousand dollar investment, *ma cherie.*"

Money! She had money that *she* had earned. Micah couldn't remember when she'd ever felt so proud or self-satisfied as when she reached out and took the check Chance handed her over his desk.

She'd known in advance, of course, what kind of profit to expect after Chance had haggled with the buyer—who had immediately fallen in love with the property. It hadn't been a hard sale, and they hadn't used a realtor which saved them a good percentage of the profits. Surely things didn't always work out so easily, but she had watched closely, and she had learned.

"Don't forget, Micah. Next time, *you* take a shot at the wheeling and dealing. We'll see if you do as well with that as you've done with fixing things up."

"I can't wait to find out myself. In fact, I've already started to scout around for our next project."

"But we just closed this one today. And don't forget, there's my second chance. Now that this is settled, you can plan our wedding. I hope you don't have plans to drag me all over town looking at do-overs for our honeymoon."

She giggled. She did want to marry him. More than anything. "Only if we check out the bedrooms first." She leaned forward to reveal a bit of cleavage, then gave him a lewd once-over. "I call the top."

"Oh, Lord," he groaned. "I've created a monster."

She raised a brow daintily, but angled her gaze just below where he sat at the desk. "You could've fooled me."

Chance got up, obviously ready to give credence to her observation, but Micah stopped him. "Wait, Chance. I have something for you."

Reaching down for her purse, she quickly took out the check she'd written the night before, then passed it across the desk. A surge of pride came with the small, but definitely self-sufficient, act.

He didn't take it at first, his brows drawing together in that expression she knew always meant trouble. "Go ahead," she urged. "It's yours. Thirteen thousand dollars. Now we're settled."

He shook his head. "I can't take that. It's *your* money. You earned it fair and square, Micah. Keep it."

She stood a little taller then, and her own jaw assumed a stubborn expression to match his. How dare he take the joy out of her accomplishment? Chance was going to take this money if she had to cram it down his throat.

Micah deliberately placed the check in front of him on the desk.

"You take this, Chance Renault."

"Damn it, Micah. You're going to be my wife. I'm not about to take your money."

"No? Well, then listen to this. As far as I'm concerned, Jonathon's debt would always be hanging over my head. I know that this money means nothing to you, but it means a lot to me. The last thing I want is something like this lurking in the back of my mind. It's no way to start our marriage."

"Maybe not, but I *still* don't like it. The debt was between him and me. Not you."

"I don't care. It's the principle of the matter." The smile she flashed was deliberately seductive and meant to throw him off guard. "Now if you'll excuse me, I have some errands to run. There's a dress I saw in a window that was begging to be worn for a wedding. It's beautiful, Chance. Pale mauve and tea-length, with dainty pearls and iridescent beads . . ."

She let her voice trail off as she watched the brooding scowl turn to grudging acceptance, and then to a crooked smile.

"Okay, Micah, you win this round. Part of being a good businessman is knowing when to cut your losses and move on. I'll take the money, but I *never* want this subject brought up again. No sense in beating a dead horse. From here we just go on." He reached down and opened the center drawer of his desk to pull out a small velvet pouch. "C'mere, you."

How could she have forgotten? The earrings! Eagerly she made her way behind the desk, watching Chance as he unsnapped the pouch and tumbled the earrings into his palm.

"I think it's time these were put back where they belong, don't you?" He looked down at her with the simmering expression of a man emotionally captive, one who reveled in the pleasure of his prison.

A small shiver ran through her at the sensation of his fingers stroking the lobe of her ear. Ever so carefully he worked the loops through, first one ear and then the other. She closed her eyes, memorizing this moment, knowing she would always remember this small, gentle act that for some reason was poignant, something to hold dear to her heart.

She could feel him raise the emerald drop with his fingertip, holding the stone lightly, as he had on her porch that night.

"Much better," he said in a gruff whisper.

No flowery speeches from Chance. Which suited him. Did he know how chivalrous he really was, how he melted her with his directness of emotion, his maverick sense of honor?

She opened her eyes. "You move me," she said. "With your goodness, you move me."

"Then you see things I don't, that no one else ever has. But you make me feel . . ." Chance shook his head. "I don't know what it is, Micah. But somehow you've always managed to bring out the best in me."

"Maybe I do. But you're forgetting something very important."

"What's that?"

"If it wasn't in you to begin with, I couldn't bring it out."

She lay her head against the broadness of his chest then, and his arms came around to hold her tightly against him. One hand slid up her back only to feather a soothing caress against her cheek before stroking the emerald which dangled beside her ear.

Micah's gaze swung upward, encompassing the expanse of the bank. Had life ever been so glorious? Could it have possibly turned out more right?

The sun reflected brilliant sparks of fire off the diamond-and-emerald engagement ring on her finger. The dress she'd told Chance about was her next stop as soon as she made this deposit and tidied up some untidy business.

She tried not to take too much pleasure in what she felt compelled to do.

The emeralds at her ears swung gaily to and fro as she paced her steps to the bank's entrance. Her stomach was starting to give her fits as she silently ran through her lines to be delivered to the esteemed Mr. Fields. Now that she was coming in on her own terms, she was going to make sure he was squirming before she was through. If she could intimidate him enough with the threat of sullying his reputation, maybe he'd leave some other woman alone.

Micah took several deep, steadying breaths to prepare herself, trying to ignore the sweating of her palms, and the small quiver in her legs as she strode closer to Ian Fields' office.

Thelma looked up from her secretarial desk when Micah cleared her throat. "Micah, hello! It's been so long since I've seen you. At least four months."

"That's about right. I just stopped by to make a deposit and thought I'd say hello to Ian. Is he in?"

The gray-haired lady suddenly darted her eyes in either direction, as though looking for spies. She peered up over the rims of her glasses, and gestured Micah closer.

"You haven't heard?" Thelma whispered.

"Heard what?"

"Mr. Fields is no longer with us."

"You're kidding," Micah blurted out. "Ian's been with the bank for over twenty years. And he's not due to retire until—"

Thelma immediately made a hushing motion as Micah's voice carried in the surrounding area.

"Let's just say he took a cut in his pension and opted for early retirement."

Micah could only open her mouth in disbelief. Nothing came out but a small exclamation of denial. Something was wrong here. And in the back of her mind a niggling suspicion kept trying to surface while she frantically tried to drown it out. There had to be some explanation, some reason for Thelma to be acting so secretive. Some other reason than the one that was twisting her stomach into tight knots of anxiety.

"When did he leave?" she managed to get out, past the constriction in her throat.

"About a month after your last visit. İt was very unexpected. A lot of talking was going on behind closed doors. Mr. Fields delivered his resignation to the board of directors and left almost immediately. That's all I know. There's a lot of speculation, but the staff wasn't really informed about anything, not even me. They kept it pretty vague." She motioned Micah a little closer and whispered conspiratorially, "Word has it he was ousted for unprofessional conduct during office hours."

Micah shut her eyes, trying to ignore the way her hair was prickling at the nape of her neck, and the dizzy sensation wrapping itself around her brain. Fuzzy, keep it fuzzy. She shouldn't start imagining things. Try not to put two and two together—that he just happened to leave soon after the incident . . . that Chance just happened to be there right after it happened . . . that Chance was on the bank's board of directors . . . that she had caught him in the middle of a heated call that morning.

"Micah, are you all right?" Thelma got up, her face showing maternal concern as Micah opened her eyes again. She struggled to steady the awkward tilt of the room.

"Oh, fine, Thelma. Just fine . . . I . . . I have to go now. It was nice seeing you again . . . Goodbye."

She turned as quickly as she dared with the buzzing in her ears making everything seem not quite real. A few people greeted her, and the best she could muster was a vague nod as she headed for . . . where? Her car, right? But then . . . where?

She got in the car and just drove. Not sure where she was going, not even able to think past Thelma's words which kept repeating themselves in her head.

A horn blared and instinctively she slammed on her brakes. Somebody whizzed past, and yelled out the window, "Learn to drive, you idiot!"

The near collision left her shaking. She had to get off the road. Driving was no place to take her confusion, her numbness, her rising anger that her suspicions were possibly true.

She had to talk to him, she told herself. Maybe she'd understood wrong. It couldn't be the way she thought, it just couldn't. . . .

Very carefully she drove to Chance's office. Getting out of her car, she could feel the reluctance in her to confront him, afraid of what she might learn.

"Hi, Micah! Mr. Renault just stepped out, but he should be back in a minute. Would you like to wait out here?"

She wasn't up to chatting with the vivacious Mrs. Allen. "Thanks, but I think I'll just wait in his office."

The secretary nodded and looked at her a little strangely. Micah wondered if her distress was showing. It should be—she was strung up so tight she couldn't even sit.

She let herself into Chance's office. Looking around, it seemed to reflect the man—the heavy, masculine furniture, the piles of neatly stacked papers, the expensive cigars he kept on hand for associates. Everything in order, and seeming to scream of power and control.

She couldn't stop pacing, running off the nervous energy that was begging her to trench a rut through the carpet. What if he'd done it, then what? Could she still marry him, somehow live with whatever excuses he had this time for his behavior? Could she leave Chance?

The questions were demanding answers when the door opened and shut quietly behind her. She swung around anxiously, crossing her arms protectively over her chest.

"Micah! I thought you were—"

"What do you know about Ian Fields' resignation?"

Chance had been coming toward her but now he stopped. Dead in his tracks. The hands he had outstretched in greeting dropped automatically to his sides.

"I had him fired."

Boom. He dropped the bomb. Quietly, efficiently, as though ruining someone's life had no more importance than signing a memo and filing it under 'Flies I have Swatted.' His face was impassive.

She opened her mouth. She closed it. There weren't any words she could find to express her anger and disappointment. And then Micah knew how desperately she'd been hoping the signs were wrong, that he hadn't done it after all. But he had.

"Aren't you going to say something, Micah? Berate me for being so callous, so coldhearted? Tell me what a mean thing it was to get rid of such a sweet old man?" She stared at him wide-eyed, clenching her fist and jaw in unison. He gestured to the paperweight close beside her on the desk. "Go ahead. Pick it up and throw it at me. I know you're mad. You have a right to be . . . to a point."

"You . . . you—" she sputtered, then grasped on to the core of it. She flung the words at him in sheer exasperation, gritted them out with mounting fury. "*Why*, Chance? Everything was good between us, and now *this*. Is this what I can expect from our marriage with you? Never knowing what kind of terrible secrets I'll discover next? Always having to be afraid of opening the wrong drawer or hearing something you've done that I'm ashamed of?"

"Ashamed?" He strode toward her briskly, his fist clenching and jaw working to match hers. They stood toe-to-toe, each glaring at the other. "If anyone should feel ashamed, it's Fields. Not me. Or you."

"No? Who gave you the right to play God? Since when were you so almighty pure yourself that you were in a position to pass that kind of judgment?"

"Go ahead and say whatever it is you're itching to get out, Micah. Say it straight." He kept his voice low, dangerously low.

"I'm talking about ethics, Chance. Morals."

His eyes slitted, and Micah knew she'd hit hard. Some kind of defense went up, hardening his features and deflecting her words like a bulletproof vest.

"Ethics and morals, huh? Something I wouldn't know about, right? Well, I've got news for you.

Believe it or not, those two things had a lot to do with my decision to ax Fields. Think about it, Micah. What he did . . . was it ethical? Moral? And did it possibly occur to you that something like this might have happened before, or could again with someone else? Possibly someone not as strong as yourself? In my book what he did was wrong."

She swallowed hard. Why did he have to be so sure of himself, so overbearing about it? And why, came the distressing thought, did it bother her so much that he was possibly right? Chance was too near, he had too much of a hold on her to think straight, that was it, wasn't it? Micah took a self-protective step back, the desk hitting the backs of her thighs and closing off any possible exit. His gaze was as unwavering as his apparent belief in his own rightness. He crossed his arms obstinately over his chest.

She wanted to feel angry still, but even now she could feel the splinters of her hostility diminishing, her own conviction of rightness begin to question itself.

"Are you really so sure that you made the right choice? Don't you ever have self-doubts about the things you do?"

"Sure, I have self-doubts. Not often, though. And I don't go around screwing with other people's lives the way you seem to think I do. When I *do* make those kinds of decisions, I make damn sure they're warranted. I looked into Fields' background after he fessed up about what he'd done . . . it wasn't the first time, Micah."

"You mean . . . he confessed?"

"Of course. After I led him to believe you'd already told me, he tried to get his side of the story told. He made it sound as if you'd practically begged him to accept your favors in exchange for a personal loan. And once he got going, I couldn't get the man to stop talking about the other women who he found his way clear to make loans for. For certain considerations."

Chance walked slowly now, closing the distance. He stood close, so close she had to tilt her head to meet his searching gaze. "You have no idea how I would have loved to punch him. Unfortunately I just referred him to the board and let them handle him."

Her anger at him was gone. In his own renegade way he'd protected her. And other women too. No doubt in another time Chance would have sheathed his lance into Ian or thrown down the gauntlet for a duel at dawn. Yet, she wanted to stand up for herself sometimes.

"Your protectiveness can go too far, Chance."

"Perhaps. But you'll have to tell me when it does. We've got a lot of years ahead of us—years I have no intention to waste by arguing over the small things."

He looked at her again. "How did you happen to find out about this today? Could it be that you had your own plans for vengeance now that you had some money in hand?"

Micah blushed, shamed.

He was right. She had burned for vengeance. Just as he had. But it was easier to blame him for going too far than facing up to her own hostilities.

"We're at the end of the line, *ma cherie*. With

us it's all or nothing. You've put me through hell and back, and I can't do that number anymore. Tell me, tell me now. Just where do *your* loyalties lie? With me? They have to be for this to work. That *is* what marriage is all about. Acceptance. Love. Compassion. Respect. Understanding."

Understanding.

"I try to understand you, Chance. You don't make it easy."

"What don't you understand?" He came closer, leaning his arms on either side of the desk to trap her there. She could feel her love for him bridging the confusion, far overriding the safeness, the emptiness of life without him.

"Why you go to such extremes . . . why you have to hold so tight to what you love."

He closed his eyes for a moment, and in that moment there was a hesitance in him, something she'd never witnessed before. And then he did open his eyes, revealing so much, telling all in the naked starkness of fear and pain she never would have thought to see in him, letting her see straight through, down to his very soul.

"Why?" he said. "Because I'm afraid. Afraid of losing you. Just like I lost my mother." He shook his head at the past, his shoulders stooped by the burden of it. "I loved her so much, and she died so young. I blamed myself for that. If only I'd been able to provide for her, if only I could have taken care of her . . . she might still be alive."

His pain was her pain, and compassion for what Chance must have gone through melted the last fragile barrier. She laid the palm of her hand against the lightly whiskered darkness of his cheek, and stroked.

"You can't blame yourself for that, Chance. You were young. There was nothing you could have done to make a difference."

"I suppose not, but it didn't seem that way then. All I could feel was the impotence, my inability to take care of her."

He caught her to him then, holding her so urgently, she thought he might crush her very bones. But she didn't care. Let him hold her until she was wholly his, a part of him, until they were one. She returned his embrace, hearing the words he whispered husky with need and more need against her hair.

"Don't leave me, Micah. Don't ever leave me. It would kill me inside to lose you . . . just thinking about it is more than I can stand. Losing you . . . it would be even worse than losing my mother. I know I grasp you too close, but sometimes, I swear, I can't help myself. Be patient. Give me some time to mellow . . . just enough to be sure I won't ever lose you again."

She ran her hands hungrily over his face, through his hair, clinging tight, tighter still. "Chance," she whispered fervently, "I won't leave you. I promise, I'll never leave again."

"Swear it, Micah."

"I swear it, Chance. I do swear it to you."

He rubbed his lips against her tears, then lapped at them until the salt upon his tongue sealed the vow within her mouth. Tempered by fire, they fell into the heat. Christening this haven, now home.

Epilogue

The flowers hadn't arrived yet. Chance checked the clock again—noon. Maybe he should call the florist to make sure they hadn't forgotten.

There was something about anniversaries that sent even guys like him straight down memory lane. A knock sounded, and Chance went to answer it, immediately greeted by flowers. The wrong ones.

"I didn't order these," he said, gesturing to the big white basket filled with baby's breath, daisies, pastel carnations and a stuffed bunny. "I asked for a fancy, tropical arrangement. Without a card. There's even a card attached to this."

The delivery boy shifted the basket in his arms and rechecked the address.

"This says it's for Chance Renault. Wrong person, right address. Sorry, I'll take these back."

"Wait a minute. *I'm* Chance Renault."

"Oh. Then I guess these are for you after all. Your order must have been mixed up with someone else's. I'll take it back and get the problem straightened out."

"Don't bother with it, Theo. You've delivered exactly what I requested."

Theo looked beyond Chance to Micah.

"Ms. Sinclair! It's been a long time. And you've moved. How are you doing?"

"Just fine." She smiled and took the basket. "Wonderful, in fact. But you can call me Mrs. Renault now. I've changed more than addresses in the last two years."

Chance cleared his throat. "I hate to break up this reunion, but if you don't mind, I'd like to speak with you, Micah. *Alone.*"

Micah pressed a tip into Theo's hand and bid him good-bye. Chance pulled her inside and closed the door.

"Why did you change my order?" he demanded. "I had something special picked out, something you'd—"

"Chance." Micah pressed her fingertips against his lips. "I didn't change your order. I didn't even know you were sending me flowers."

"No? Then what's this?"

He glanced at the basket, puzzled.

"For you," she said, smiling. "Happy anniversary, darling."

"Happy anniversary," he returned, reaching for her instead of the card.

Micah stepped just out of his reach, and nodded to the envelope. "Go ahead," she urged. "Open it."

Chance grumbled something about her depriving him of his husbandly rights but complied.

While he worked the envelope open, Micah reached for the stuffed bunny and wound the key attached. A music box version of Brahms' Lullaby began to filter through the room as Chance scanned the card.

"Congratulations," he read aloud. "The rabbit died."

His hand suddenly seemed unsteady, and he stared at Micah as the card sailed awkwardly to the floor.

"Congratulations," she whispered, draping her arms around his neck, "Daddy."

"Micah," he murmured. "Oh, Micah." Chance swept her into his arms, and headed for the stairs, his voice lodged somewhere between his heart and his throat. Another knock sounded at the front door but he ignored it as he moved purposefully toward the bedroom.

"Aren't we going to get that?"

"What for?" His voice sounded a little choked, and he brought her closer to his chest. "It's only some flowers. Flowers with the most important part missing."

"A card?" She smiled, and cuddled closer.

"More than a card. A message. One that says how lucky we are." He laid her down on their bed. "Besides, I think you know how it ends."

"Tell me anyway," she whispered.

"Enough talk," he said, pulling her into his arms. "Just kiss me now, *ma cherie*. Kiss the man who loves you."

THE EDITOR'S CORNER

There's something a little bit forbidden about this month's group of heroes. For one reason or another they seem to be exactly the wrong men for our heroines to fall in love with—but, of course, the six ladies involved do just that, unable as they are to resist the potent allure of these special LOVESWEPT men. And what they feared was forbidden fruit turns out to be necessary to their very existences!

In **TROPICAL HEAT**, LOVESWEPT #432, Patt Bucheister creates a noble hero named John Canada, and she puts his nobility to the test by having him fight his overwhelming passion for Salem Shepherd, the woman he'd first known as a young girl. Together they had escaped from an orphanage and forged a friendship based on trust and need. But the feelings that began to surface in John as Salem blossomed into womanhood scared him, tempted him, thrilled him—and made him realize he had to send her away. Years later Salem returns to help John when his business is in trouble, and the feelings he'd once felt for her pale in comparison to the desire he knows he can no longer fight. These two people who've shared so much find themselves swept away on a current stronger than an ocean surge, right into the arms of destiny. Patt has outdone herself in crafting a love story of immense emotional impact.

Charlotte Hughes gives her heroine something of a dilemma in **RESTLESS NIGHTS**, LOVESWEPT #433. How can Kelly Garrett get on with her life as an independent single mom, when she discovers she's falling for Macon Bridges, a man who represents so much of what she's struggled to put behind her after her first marriage failed. Macon is the successful owner of the firm she works for; he has the tendency to want to take control and do things for her that she's just learned to do for herself; he's dedicated to his job and at times allows it to take top priority in his life. Then again, the man can charm the birds from the trees and certainly knows how to send Kelly's heart into flight! But

(continued)

once this smitten lady makes up her mind to risk it all on the sexy man who's causing her too many restless nights, it's Macon who doesn't stand a chance! Charlotte's lighthearted style makes this story pure entertainment.

TEMPESTUOUS, LOVESWEPT #434, by Tami Hoag, not only describes the feisty heroine in the book, Alexandra Gianni, but also the state of the atmosphere whenever she encounters hero Christian Atherton. The sparks do fly between the aristocratic charmer who is used to having women fall at his feet not throw him to the ground, and the lovely wildcat with the haunted eyes and determined ways of a woman who has something to hide. At first Christian sees winning Alex as a challenge, until he becomes thoroughly enchanted by the spirited woman he yearns to know all about. His wicked reputation seems in jeopardy as he longs only to soothe Alex's sorrow and shower her with tenderness. But not until Alex convinces herself she deserves to be cherished can she accept Christian's gift of love. This poignant romance features several characters from two of Tami's previous books, **RUMOR HAS IT**, #304, and **MAN OF HER DREAMS**, #331, the most notable character of which is hero Christian, whose love story you've asked Tami for in your letters. Enjoy!

Joan Elliott Pickart's **TO LOVE AND TO CHERISH**, LOVESWEPT #435, opens with a dramatic scene that won't fail to grip you. Imagine meeting a stranger in the foggy cocoon of night on a deserted beach. In a moment of yearning desperation, imagine yourself surrendering to him body and soul, then running off without ever learning his name! Heroine Alida Hunter was lost in her grief until she met the man with the summer-sky eyes. But she knew he was a fantasy, a magical gift she could never keep. Paul-Anthony Payton couldn't forget the mysterious woman who'd bewitched him then vanished, and he vowed to find her. She'd filled him with hope that night on the beach, but when he finally does find her, his hopes are dashed by her denial of what they'd shared.

(continued)

Alida's fear of loving and losing terrifies her and prevents her from believing in Paul-Anthony's promises. But the more she tells herself he's the forbidden lover of her dreams, the more Paul-Anthony makes her dreams become reality. Once again Joan delivers a powerful love story LOVESWEPT fans will treasure.

Judy Gill casts another memorable character in the role of hero in **MOONLIGHT MAN,** LOVESWEPT #436. Judy orchestrates perfectly this romance between Sharon Leslie, a gifted musician in whose heart the music has all but died, and Marc Duval, a man who's endured an unbearable tragedy and learned to find beauty and peace in the music he plays. Marc sees how Sharon is drawn to and yet tormented by the melodies he sends to her on the wind—as she is to his mesmerizing kisses. He knows she doubts herself as a woman even as he awakens her to pleasure beyond anything she's ever known. But until he can earn Sharon's trust, he can't know why she keeps turning away from him—and once she does trust him, he realizes he will have to confess the black secret of his own past. Caught up in the rebirth of the music inside her, Sharon revels in her feelings for Marc, but it all comes crashing down on her when she discovers the truth about the man she now loves with all her heart. Judy gives us a shining example of how true love conquers all in this wonderfully touching romance.

Fayrene Preston continues her SwanSea Place series with **JEOPARDY,** LOVESWEPT #437. Judging by the hero's name alone, Amarillo Smith, you can expect this to be one sultry, exciting, dangerous romance that only Fayrene can write—and you won't be disappointed. Heroine Angelica DiFrenza is surprised and intrigued when private investigator Amarillo, her brother's partner, asks her to dinner—the broodingly handsome detective had always seemed to avoid her deliberately. But when they finally end up alone together, the passion flares hotter than a blast furnace, and they both realize there's no going back. Amarillo couldn't deny

(continued)

what he'd felt for so long, but the time wasn't right. He was desperate to protect Angelica from the danger that threatened her life, and he needed a clear head and un-involved emotions to do it. But Amarillo's tantalizing kisses create a fever in Angelica's blood and the maelstrom of uncivilized hunger they'd suspected brewed between them rages out of control. You'll want to follow these two along on their journey of discovery, which, of course, leads them to beautiful SwanSea Place.

We promised you more information about our LOVESWEPT hotline, and here it is! If you'd like to reach your favorite LOVESWEPT authors by phone, all you have to do is dial 1-900-896-2505 between October 1 and December 31 to hear exciting mes-sages and up-to-the-minute information. You *may* call and get the author in person! Not only will you be able to get the latest news and gossip, but just by calling and leaving your name you will be entered into our Romantic Getaway Sweepstakes, where you'll have a chance to win a grand prize of a free week for two to Paris! Each call you make will cost you 95¢ per min-ute, and winners of the contest will be chosen at random from the names gathered. More detailed in-struction and rules will appear in the backs of our November, December, and January LOVESWEPTs. But the number will be operational beginning on October 1 and ending on December 31!

Get your dialing fingers ready!

Sincerely,

Susann Brailey

Susann Brailey
Editor
LOVESWEPT
Bantam Books
666 Fifth Avenue
New York, NY 10103

FOREVER LOVESWEPT
SPECIAL KEEPSAKE EDITION OFFER
SELECTION FORM

Choose from these special Loveswepts by your favorite authors. Please write a 1 next to your first choice, a 2 next to your second choice. Loveswept will honor your preference as inventory allows.

♡ ♡ ♡ *Loveswept*®

_____BAD FOR EACH OTHER   Billie Green

_____NOTORIOUS   Iris Johansen

_____WILD CHILD   Suzanne Forster

_____A WHOLE NEW LIGHT   Sandra Brown

_____HOT TOUCH   Deborah Smith

_____ONCE UPON A TIME...GOLDEN
    THREADS   Kay Hooper

Attached are 15 hearts and the selection form which indicates my choices for my special hardcover Loveswept "Keepsake Edition." Please mail my book to:

NAME:_____

ADDRESS:_____

CITY/STATE:_____ZIP:_____

Offer open only to residents of the United States, Puerto Rico and Canada. Void where prohibited, taxed, or restricted. Allow 6 - 8 weeks after receipt of coupons for delivery. Offer expires January 15, 1991. You will receive your first choice as inventory allows; if that book is no longer available, you'll receive your second choice, etc.